EMMA OF IRAN

To Diane

T. Marion Dodge

© 2017 T. Marion Dodge
All rights reserved.

ISBN: 0999413570
ISBN 13: 9780999413579

CHAPTER ONE

April 15, 1988, Tehran, Iran

The letter was in a plain yellow envelope. It was obviously an official letter. Emma held it in her hand and started to shiver. It had been abruptly handed to her by the evil one through the cracked door. She had seen this man before: he had been one of the men who had recruited Hamid. She even knew his name, but she referred to him only as the evil one. She had a strong sense about people and had hated him from the start.

Even through the barely opened door she could smell the strong aroma of alcohol, strictly forbidden in Iran, but still often secretly enjoyed by men in power. Emma couldn't interpret the twisted smile he gave her as he handed her the letter, and quickly closed the door.

She dropped to her knees and found the strength to open the envelope. She spread the letter on the floor, her hands shaking too much to hold it. It stated simply, "Commander Hamid Aroundami has been reported missing and presumed dead in the glorious fight to save our country."

She was not good at reading Persian script, but the 'dead' and 'Hamid Aroundami' parts were very clear. Her tears soaked the note below her. She'd always known this day was possible, but somehow thought it would never happen to her Hamid. He was different... he would be protected... he would surely come back to her.

Moments later the door burst open and the evil one was standing in front of her. She jumped to her feet and screamed in Persian, "Get out!" He laughed as he looked directly at her, and shut the door behind him. The smell of gunpowder, sweat and alcohol hit her. She could not understand why he was there because no other men were allowed in the house without Hamid being present...It was unspeakable. But there he was.

He grabbed her arm that was pointing at the door, and, with his other hand, pulled a piece of paper from his pocket and said in drunken Persian, "Your husband is dead. You and I will agree to a sighe for the next three days." He put the marriage contract on the hall table, flattening it open with his hand.

Emma stood there, stunned. He was expecting her to agree to a temporary marriage with him so that they could have sex under the blessing of Islamic tradition.

"I will not!" she declared in Persian. Her mind was on fire. The initial crushing heartbreak had shifted to sheer terror.

He gripped her arm tighter. The sickening, smiling scowl left no doubt what he was about to do. He was a man who always got what he wanted.

"Please leave," Emma begged, trying to free her arm, but he would not listen.

"Sign this!" He scowled, pointing to the contract on the table. "Or I will kill you now, and your two baby girls will be left alone in this world."

Mentioning her two year old twins sleeping in the next room would be the biggest mistake of his life.

"I will not, you filthy pig. Leave now!"

He pulled her closer, his other arm now wrapped around her waist. She could feel his erection pressed up against her and struggled frantically to break away.

He loosened his grip and slapped her hard on the face, knocking her to the floor. He hovered above her, pinning her to the ground with his huge hand on her neck and bent down inches from her, his filthy alcohol breath in her face. "You will sign the document, you disgusting American whore. Now, or after."

He reached for her chador and viciously tore it, ripping it from her head and partially exposing her breast. In his drunken state he lost his balance and fell to his knees.

Emma scrambled to her feet, kicking and slapping. He, too, rose and they crashed into the kitchen.

Emma fought with everything she had, but the evil one was almost twice her size. He was laughing and playing with her like a cat with a mouse. He slapped her again and again, then pulled his arm back and punched her in the face. The force of it caused her to stumble across the kitchen and into the counter, where she found herself looking directly at the knife block.

In one viciously graceful motion she pulled out a knife, turned, and with a primal scream threw it at the evil one with all her might, the way she had been trained. The knife struck him dead center, chest high, just below the breastbone. He had already pulled off his jacket and was down to his white T-shirt, with his pants down around his knees. With a shocked expression he looked down at the handle of the knife coming out of his chest, his T-shirt instantly soaked with blood. He looked up at Emma as he dropped to his knees, his mouth moving but no words coming out.

Catching her breath, she stood looking at him a moment. Then she calmly walked over, grabbed him by the hair and bent down close to his face. She stared at his dying eyes and in a clear, steady voice said, "You were killed by an American woman, you sadistic son of a whore."

She let go of his hair, and Farzad Rostami, the second-highest ranking officer in the Iranian Republican Guard, fell limp to the floor, his last moments sealing his eternal damnation.

CHAPTER TWO

November 3rd, 1979—Nine Years Earlier

Yasmin rested in her sterile hospital bed with Emma by her side, a few tissues and paper cups next to her on the bedside table. Tubes ran from an IV into her veins. She was exhausted from the constant pain.

They were in a Seattle hospital that offered an experimental treatment that seemed to have promise for her cancer. Emma and Yasmin had flown to Seattle together, leaving her husband Eric at the embassy in Iran to deal with the turmoil brewing there. He was a chief diplomat, and the only American-born person in the embassy who could speak fluent Persian.

Early in 1979, the US-supported Shah of Iran and his regime had fallen. His nemesis, the Ayatollah Khomeini, had returned from exile to lead the country. Relations with the US were deteriorating, and when the Shah was allowed to move to the United States in October for cancer treatment, animosity and anger toward the US took an ominous turn. Protesters surrounded the US embassy in Iran around the clock, demanding the return of the Shah to stand trial.

Yasmin watched the TV above her bed, tracking the ongoing news bulletins about Iran as the medicines poured into her veins. It seemed to be helping, she thought. At least there wasn't as much pain. She looked at her young Emma and smiled, very proud of her lovely daughter in her beautiful hijab. Emma was truly turning into a woman in front of her eyes. Yasmin knew that it was unlikely she would see her daughter on her wedding day—the treatment might give her months, but certainly not years.

Yasmin's mind swirled in a drug-induced dream world. Her thoughts ranged from clear-headed reflection to a surreal blur of confusing visions. She did not want to die. It was not so much fear of her own death, but fear of leaving behind an unmarried daughter who still had so much to learn about life. She did not want Emma to fall into a western lifestyle. She and Eric had had many discussions and arguments about the topic, but ultimately they had decided that Emma would choose for herself which of her parents' worlds to join: Eric's American culture, or Yasmin's Iranian one.

Yasmin could not help but smile at her daughter's maturity, as the girl sat straight-backed in the hospital chair. The small family had spent much of Emma's fifteen years traveling from embassy to embassy, and the diverse cultures she'd been exposed to had helped her grow into a woman beyond her years.

But Yasmin worried about what would happen upon her death. Eric was certainly a capable father, but how was he to know anything about what Emma's Iranian side really meant?

Her thoughts were interrupted by a gentle knock on the door. The doctor entered, a middle-aged woman of Iranian decent who specialized in breast cancer. Yasmin had learned that she, too, had family in Iran. With her that morning was a young, strikingly handsome Middle Eastern-looking man with a notepad and a quiet demeanor. He stood back, observing the doctor's movements. Yasmin watched him through sleepy eyes as the doctor checked her chart and reviewed the treatment plan.

"Your numbers look better, Yasmin. How do you feel?" asked the doctor.

"A little better," said Yasmin, "But sometimes I have been aching in my bones. It is hard to sleep at night; I think maybe the bed is too firm."

The doctor didn't comment, but continued to look at the chart.

The young man seemed distracted by the TV. When he turned to look at Yasmin she asked him, in Persian, "You are Iranian, no?"

He looked at the doctor as if seeking permission to speak, but the doctor was focused on Yasmin's IV.

"Yes, Iranian," he said in English. "On a student visa, one year ago I come."

"Perhaps you should meet my daughter. What is your name?" Yasmin asked, shifting to English as well.

"Mother!" Emma blurted.

Emma was looking down at her hands, seemingly appalled by her mother's directness.

"My sweet girl, I am dying. I get to do whatever I want at this point," looking back at the young man, who was obviously uncomfortable with the conversation.

He glanced at Emma, then looked directly at Yasmin and said in a proud voice, "I am Hamid.".

"Hamid, this is my daughter Emma. Emma, this is Hamid."

The two made awkward eye contact. Emma then stood and busied herself cleaning Yasmin's tray. Hamid shifted back to focusing on the doctor's movements. She seemed to be satisfied and was preparing to leave.

Another news flash appeared on the TV screen, this one more ominous:

"CRISIS IN IRAN. US EMBASSY IN PERIL"

Yasmin pointed at the remote, "Emma, please turn the TV up."

Emma turned the volume up. "We turn now to the situation in Iran at the US embassy," a newscaster said. "There have been sporadic reports of individuals attempting to enter the grounds. What has been mostly peaceful up until now appears to be turning into a more chaotic scene."

The doctor reached for the remote and turned the TV off. "Yasmin, you really should avoid all stress," she said, "the news isn't that important."

"My husband is a diplomat in the embassy," said Yasmin. "It is a stress I cannot avoid."

The doctor handed the remote back to Emma. "My apologies. I didn't know." She gently patted Yasmin's arm, then turned and nodded to Hamid and they both left the room.

CHAPTER THREE

As the doctor and Hamid left Yasmin's hospital room, Hamid glanced briefly in Emma's direction and was able to catch her eye just for a moment. She was the most beautiful woman he had ever seen, and he was hoping that his student shift in this ward would continue for a while.

It was good to be around people from his own country. It was hard to know how the embassy problem was going to affect him, but he feared the worst.

As Hamid continued on his rounds with the doctor, he could not stop thinking of Emma. He had never even been on a date. There were women back home that he thought liked him, but he had been too caught up in his studies to be interested. At first, his family wanted him to study in Iran, but the exchange program that the Shah had set up with the US was very beneficial. On top of that, the turmoil in Iran was intensifying; people were disappearing in the night. His parents decided he would be safer in America, so Hamid went. Although he would be able to get into the best universities in Iran, getting into a major US college was appealing too, and the job offers when he returned would be endless.

His parents were pushing for him to be a doctor, but Hamid was more interested in tinkering with equipment and electronics. Most of the equipment used in Iran was American-made, in virtually every sector of the economy, and being trained by American teachers to work with American equipment made sense. When the acceptance letter arrived from the University of Washington's School of Medicine, it settled the discussion; it was simply too good to pass up.

Although Hamid loved his studies, they didn't leave him much of a social life. But he really couldn't understand the American men around him in school anyway; they seemed to be most impressed with the ones who could drink the most beer or who had the most stories about being with women. It was a world he found confusing and immoral. He often wondered how America was so successful, when so many of the students spent more time focusing on the next party than on their studies.

The day after seeing Emma, Hamid found out that he had been assigned to another section of the hospital for the next month. He would not be anywhere near the cancer ward. Though disappointed, he decided that it was God's will.

CHAPTER FOUR

Hamid walked through the courtyard on his usual route to the library. The fallen leaves of the approaching season padded his walk along the winding path. He steadily walked up the dozen or so steps to the main entrance. It was a stunningly beautiful building, something that only early twentieth century architects seemed capable of designing.

Passing through the huge, ornate doors leading into the library study hall was his signal to shift his brain; to alert his senses so that he could focus entirely on his studies.

He found his favorite desk, arranged his books and settled in, starting with organic chemistry. Most students feared and loathed the course. For him, however, it was an explanation of God. The formulas and models representing compounds and elements came to him immediately. He could imagine them in 3D, shift his view from one side to the other of an impossibly complex tetrahedral molecule, and even rearrange it while it drifted in his thoughts. But he had stopped trying to explain his thoughts to his professor, who seemed to imply that what he was suggesting was impossible for the human brain.

Hamid was staring at the book, lost in his thoughts, when a whispered 'hello' startled him out of his trance. He turned, and saw Emma behind him, shyly smiling and looking at him with her striking green eyes. He stared her with his mouth agape, not knowing what to say.

Emma glanced downward, then lifted her eyes and murmured, "Can we go somewhere and talk?"

Hamid looked around. Speaking to Emma was inappropriate, he was sure. There must be someone watching. When he convinced himself that no one was paying attention to them, he nodded and stood. Emma led the way through the great old ornate doors and into the hallway, out of the silent study room.

"I'm sorry to interrupt," Emma began as they found a quiet bench and sat down, Hamid sitting body-width away from her. "I wanted to tell you that I was very embarrassed by my mother's introduction."

"But how did you know where to find me?" Hamid said, completely perplexed.

Emma gave him a clever look. "I asked some of the other students where you might study, and they told me maybe the library. I have been walking around to find you." She lowered her eyes, seemingly embarrassed to be admitting such a thing. But Hamid couldn't help but notice her smile. More of a smirk actually, just one side of her beautiful mouth turned up slightly.

Emma continued, "I know this would be most inappropriate if we were in Iran, but I think our situations are unique. Allah would understand."

Hamid spoke in an authoritative tone. "But I think you are much too young to be here, and you should not be here alone."

Emma stared at him defiantly, a spark of anger in her eyes. "This is America. I get to go where I want, and my age has nothing to do with it. I am old enough to be here."

"But I do not think that Allah would approve. You should be with a family member when you are out."

"If God is watching, then you will mind your manners, I suppose," she retorted with a playful smirk.

Hamid smiled back at her, admiring her quick wit. But he was still unsure about sitting with such a young, beautiful woman who was not related to him.

There were so few Iranian women on campus, and American women just did not interest Hamid. Their uninhibited behavior made him uncomfortable. He was trying his best to adjust, but when he was around Americans he often ended up just keeping quiet, and he was mostly ignored by both men and women.

Emma snapped him out of his thoughts. "We could go for a walk," she suggested. "The school grounds are very beautiful, and it is a lovely morning. My mother is sleeping, I do not need to be there for a while."

Hamid looked at her, his mind racing. Being alone with a woman much younger had to be a sin. Perhaps Allah was trying to somehow help them to be together? After thinking long enough to make both of them uncomfortable, he just shrugged and gave her a reluctant nod.

It was a very pleasant early November day, and unseasonably warm. A few leaves clung to the maple trees lining the walkway, despite the looming winter. Towering evergreen trees that must have been a hundred years old were scattered throughout the campus.

They walked in silence, until Emma said, "Is it just me, or are people staring at us?"

Hamid thought for a moment, then said, "It must be your beauty. I normally don't notice people looking at me so much." He had just been stating a fact, but almost immediately he realized the involuntary compliment.

Emma blushed, then said "Well, you are very handsome. I think maybe it is you they are looking at."

He had no idea how to respond. Maybe she was joking. He just looked straight ahead in silence, thinking it was dangerous for him to open his mouth.

A couple walked by and gave them angry stares.

"It can be odd at times here. Often I miss Tehran," said Emma, once out of earshot of the staring couple.

"Yes, I feel that very often," said Hamid, "but most of my time is work or study, so in a way it is good for me. I'm able to focus more on my study. How is your mother?"

Emma sighed. "It is very hard. She is very sick."

"What about your father? Will he be coming to take care of you?"

"I hope so. Right now he's still in Iran, at the US embassy. He is a very important diplomat there, and things are difficult. We came back a couple of months ago for treatment. He should be coming soon, once things settle down there. Or if my mother gets worse, he will come."

"So he is American?"

"Yes, I am half American and half Iranian."

"Well, your Iranian side is most beautiful," Hamid said, then averted his eyes, aghast at his own words.

Emma blushed, looking around at the trees. "And what of your parents," she asked. "Are they in Iran?"

Hamid shook his head, looking down. "They were taken in the middle of the night six months ago, by the Savak."

She stopped walking. "I am so sorry. That is awful."

"It was not God's will; the people that took them were godless. It was the work of the devil. I cannot describe my sadness. My parents were very gentle and loving people. Their only sin was not liking the Shah."

They continued walking in silence, eventually coming to the student union building.

"Perhaps we could go for a soda? I am very thirsty," said Emma, breaking the silence.

They entered the building to find a huge gathering around a TV. The room was mostly silent as people listened to the blaring news.

The newscaster said, "Once again, the US embassy in Tehran has been overrun by a huge mob. It is unknown at this time who these people are or their intentions. The status of the embassy staff is unknown at this point. We understand that there are up to sixty Americans inside the embassy."

The television showed scenes of chaos. Ayatollah Khomeini posters were being pasted on walls. Angry men shouted slogans: "God is Great! Death to America!" A man in a collared shirt and a hastily prepared blindfold was being paraded through the chaos. Emma stood stock still, her face draining of all color. Then she turned to Hamid and said, "I believe that is my father."

CHAPTER FIVE

As they entered Yasmin's ward, Hamid said, "I should not be with you when we see your mother. I think it is most disrespectful." They had come directly from the student union building, Emma anxious to tell her mother the news.

"Please come with me," said Emma, "I think she will understand."

As they approached Yasmin's room they saw a flurry of activity, with nurses and doctors coming and going. A nurse recognized Emma and called out, "Emma!" She approached with a face full of sadness and sympathy.

"Your mother has fallen into a coma. We are doing our best, but her situation is not good. I am so sorry."

They entered the room to find Molly Andrade sitting next to Yasmin. Molly was Yasmin's college friend, who still lived in Seattle. Yasmin had stayed in touch with Molly over the years, and Emma had been staying with Molly while Yasmin was getting treatment.

The TV was on in the corner but the volume was off, and visuals on the screen were telling the story of the chaos in Tehran.

"Oh, Emma." Molly stood to greet her with a hug.

Hamid stood near the door while Emma approached her mother. She shifted some of the tubes so that she could hold her mother's hands. She felt a slight squeeze, then her mother's hand fell away. The monitor showed that her heart had stopped. A loud beeping came from the machine.

The doctor and nurse came forward and Emma backed away from the bed as they tried to resuscitate Yasmin. She knew it was fruitless; she had felt the moment life left her mother.

Emma stared at the body that only moments before had been her mother. The room swirled in front of her. She heard voices, but no words registered in her mind. It didn't feel real, it couldn't be real, but it seemed to be happening.

Molly was speaking, but Emma wasn't listening. She turned to Hamid and said, "Do you know who can perform a ghusl? I am not familiar with the Islamic community here; there has been no time."

Hamid said, "Let me call the mosque I attend." He quickly left the room.

The doctor was satisfying himself that the woman on the table was indeed dead. The doctor then whispered something to the nurse and she pulled the sheet up over Yasmin's face.

Emma said, "Please, can you all leave for a few minutes?"

The doctor studied the young woman's face. Then he looked at the nurse and Molly, and said "Yes, of course." He and the nurse left the room. Molly stayed by the bed.

"Molly, please give me a moment alone with my mother," Emma said. Molly nodded, wiped tears away, and stood. She hugged Emma and left the room, passing Hamid on her way out.

"The mosque can do it," Hamid said. "We will have to arrange it with the hospital. It can be difficult, I am told. The mosque said they could be here to pick her up in one hour."

"Thank you, Hamid. I know I have not done everything properly—I did not think she would die so quickly. Perhaps we could angle the bed to face Mecca, and I can say a prayer."

They made the adjustments and Hamid moved to the back of the room. He knelt and bowed deeply as Emma pulled the sheet back from Yasmin's face. Emma retrieved Yasmin's hijab from a side table and gently put it on, the way Yasmin liked. She then adjusted Yasmin's hands so they overlapped on her chest. Emma stepped back and bowed her head, with her own hands in prayer position, and began.

"O Allah, I bear witness for my mother Yasmin that there is no God but Allah. Forgive my mother Yasmin and elevate her station among those who are guided. Send her along the path of those who have come before, and forgive us and her, O lord of the world. Enlarge her grave and shed light upon her in it."

Emma bowed deeply, lifted her head, and slowly covered Yasmin's face with the sheet once again.

CHAPTER SIX

"We will need to pick up my mother's body today to take it to the mosque for preparation," Emma said to the woman at the nurse's station.

The nurse looked up at Emma. "Honey, we can't do that. Your mother's body needs to go to the cold room downstairs. Then the mortician will take it to the mortuary, and from there they handle everything. Now if you just have a seat, we will take care of everything. Don't you worry."

Emma didn't move. "It is Islamic law," she said quietly. "It is required that a ghusl be performed and that she be buried within twenty-four hours in a Muslim cemetery."

The nurse's eyes narrowed. "Well, I'm very sorry honey, but this is a Christian nation and it just doesn't work that way." She turned her attention to a file on her desk.

Emma glared at the woman. As Molly walked up with a folder in her hand, Emma said to the nurse, "My mother's body will be leaving this hospital in one hour's time, with the people from the mosque. Her body will not be going with your mortician. If you are not authorized to release her into my care, I need to talk to the person that has the authority. Now, please."

Without saying a word, Molly pulled a health directive from the folder and handed it to the nurse, who looked at it and rose from her chair. She went to a back office with the directive in her hand.

An hour later, they were on their way to the mosque with Yasmin's body.

Emma and Hamid joined Molly in her car, following the hearse. "I can contact my friend in the CIA and see if I can get a message through to your father," Molly said. "Perhaps you can write me a message to pass along? To tell him about your mother. Or if it's too much right now, I can do it."

"Thank you so much. If you could write the note that would be most helpful." Emma smiled sadly and gently patted Molly's arm as they continued down the road. "The message will get to my father. It is a foundation of Islam that relatives of the dead be notified—this will be honored, I have no doubt."

When word got out at the mosque of the strong young woman whose mother's body was coming for her ghusl, there was no shortage of volunteers to assist. By the time Emma and Hamid and the men from the mosque arrived with Yasmin's body, the washing room was set up and ready and three of the more experienced women were prepared to begin the procedure.

Yasmin's body was carried into the washing room by the men who had picked her up at the hospital. They carefully laid her on the table, then left. Hamid went with them. One of the women closed the door behind them.

"May I stay?" asked Emma.

"Of course," said one of the women, sadly smiling at Emma.

Emma sat in a chair to the side where she had a view of the procedure. Each of the women came to her in turn with their hands in prayer position, acknowledging her, then returned to the table.

The women carefully removed Yasmin's clothing and jewelry and placed a privacy cloth across her body. Gently and methodically they washed her body from head to toe three times, starting each washing with, "In the name of Allah."

After the third washing, her hair was washed, combed, braided in three braids, and placed behind her back. Some camphor was sprinkled on her body and she was carefully dried. They then opened the package for the shroud, which consisted of a number of sheets and ties and headdresses, and expertly wrapped her body.

Although Islamic tradition required that Yasmin be buried in an all-Muslim cemetery, there were none available in the entire state of Washington. However, an agreement had been worked out between the mosque and a local cemetery to open a secluded section for Muslim burials.

A plot near an evergreen tree was available. Emma was very appreciative of the lovely spot. The cemetery official assured her that her mother properly faced Mecca. The tree nearby would provide shade for her. Yasmin had never liked being in the sun.

Emma asked the Imam if he would invite the entire congregation to the burial, including the women, and he agreed. She also requested that there be no wailing or shrieking. Emma knew the Koran was clear on this point, and that Allah would not approve.

Although Yasmin was not known to the people in the mosque, Emma's tragic story over the last couple of days was quickly circulating, and everyone wanted to show their support. Hamid stood next to Emma at the grave, along with the Imam and the men who would lower the casket. Molly and her husband Jim stood together a few feet behind. Emma had borrowed a black dress from Molly, and Hamid, like the other men, wore a black suit and tie.

As the hearse arrived with the casket, two lines of men quietly formed. A steady stream of cars was arriving—mosque members who wanted to show their respect. New men silently filled in the gaps in the line. The men removed the casket from the hearse and expertly lifted it to their shoulders, then steadily passed it shoulder to shoulder down the line of men in silence, until it reached the gravesite.

The prayers were read in traditional Islamic fashion. Emma stood stoically next to Hamid as Yasmin was lowered into the earth.

Emma then slowly walked over to the mound of dirt next to the grave, trying to stay composed as she tossed three handfuls of dirt on top of the coffin. She stepped back and Hamid did the same, followed by the Imam. Molly and Jim followed their lead. Again a line formed, and each person at the funeral, silently and one by one, tossed three handfuls of dirt into the grave.

Emma watched as her new community helped her bury her mother, one handful at a time. She could feel God's presence as never before.

She silently stood watching as tears flowed down her face. She was comforted because she knew that only God gives life and only God takes it away, at a time that he decides.

CHAPTER SEVEN

Emma looked at Hamid as they sat in the back seat of Molly and Jim's car. He turned and looked at her with strong and sympathetic eyes. This was the man she would spend the rest of her life with; she had known it from the moment they met. Somehow her mother had known that too.

Normally the mourners would go to the house of the deceased after the funeral, but since Yasmin had died in the hospital, and since she and Emma had no home yet in Seattle, it was agreed that the mosque dining hall would be the best location for the meal following the burial.

People who had not been able to make the service were busy setting up the feast. As Emma stood near the door of the large dining hall a steady stream of people arrived, all with gifts and food in hand. The women all greeted Emma with a handshake and a hug. She didn't know any of them, but it felt like they had been family forever, and their generosity and kindness touched her deeply.

Her thoughts turned to what to do next. It would be impossible for her to continue stay with Molly and Jim now that her mother had died; they had no concept of Islam. Although they had been kind to her, she needed her faith now more than ever. What if she and Hamid were to join in a sighe?

Emma knew there would be a three day mourning period, but she felt that her dilemma required immediate attention, and she hoped Allah would understand.

She liked the way the Imam had led the prayers at the funeral, and since he was the leader of the local mosque she felt he was the best one to discuss her living arrangements with.

On arrival at the mosque she had asked to speak with him directly, which was highly unusual, but given the unusual circumstances, the Imam had agreed. They entered his office together and he motioned for her to sit on a chair. He sat behind his desk. The door was wide open.

"Thank you for meeting me on such short notice," Emma began.

"Yes, yes," said the Imam in english. "You have been through much sorrow, I can only hope I can be of some help."

Emma started right in. "Thank you. I am fifteen years old, I have lost my mother, and my father is being held in the embassy in Iran. I cannot go back to Iran now, and I have no relatives here. I have stayed with my mother's friend Molly since we came here for treatment, and she would gladly allow me to stay, but I am uncomfortable staying with her for an indefinite time, since she is not a Muslim. I would like you to allow Hamid and I to join in a temporary marriage so that I may live with him under the blessing of Islam, at least until my father returns from Iran. We can state in the sighe that it will be a non-sexual sighe, that it be done only by the grace of Allah, and only if Allah, too, shall see the wisdom of the sighe between us."

The Imam stared at Emma with his mouth open. He'd never heard such a suggestion, and this was coming from a woman, a fifteen year old, whose mother had just died. He muttered, in Persian, "I... what of Hamid's parents? Do you have their blessing?"

Emma firmly responded back in Persian, "His parents were taken six months ago by the Savak police in the middle of the night. Hamid has not heard from any of his remaining siblings or cousins. He fears the worst."

The Imam sat there thinking, tapping a pencil on the desk in front of him, staring straight at Emma. "And what of Hamid? Why is he not here to discuss this? I should be speaking with him."

"He is not aware of my plans. But I believe he is a good Muslim and will agree."

The Imam raised his eyebrows. "Is your father a Muslim?"

"Yes," said Emma. "He is American, but he converted many years ago so the marriage with my mother received a family blessing. But he is not so serious, I think. He is a diplomat in the American embassy—he is one of the hostages. My mother's friend Molly is my legal guardian, at least until my father returns."

The Imam took a heavy breath and blew it out. "And what would your father want you to do?"

"He would want what my mother would want. We did not have a traditional Islamic family. This was confusing at times for me, until I became clear that Islam was the direction that I wanted to go with my life."

The Imam thought further. It might be best to stop asking questions... the more he asked, the more complicated it was getting. Besides, the clarity and truth in Emma's voice demanded respect. Frowning, he said, "I need to think. Please send Hamid to discuss this with me. I need to speak to a higher authority as well. Please stay with your friend Molly until I can be sure of the right thing to do. The sighe is an Islamic agreement, not a legal document. If she is your guardian, I believe you will need her approval."

Emma was disappointed, but at least the Imam hadn't said no. She rose from her chair. "Thank you for meeting with me; I appreciate your wisdom and consideration. I will inform Hamid that you wish to speak with him. I have not mentioned this to him, so it will come as a surprise." She gave the Imam a subtle bow of respect before she left the room.

CHAPTER EIGHT

"Emma, you can't do that! You're only fifteen years old—you need to be with an adult." Molly's voice sounded shocked and her eyes were wide. They were in Molly's living room and Emma had just explained her plans.

"Hamid is an adult. He is nineteen. It will not be sexual; it will be spelled out in the sighe," Emma patiently explained.

Molly shook her head. "I know this is hard, Emma. Your mother just died. But it is no time to start making rash decisions. You hardly know Hamid, and I'm not even sure it would be legal. I should be the one that takes care of you. It is what Yasmin would wish."

Emma's voice rose. "You do not know what my mother would wish. She introduced Hamid and me. She always had a strong sense about these things. It is what I believe she would have wanted."

Molly could hardly contain herself. "You are fifteen years old! You simply cannot do this!"

Emma sighed and lowered her head, then looked directly at Molly. "I trust Hamid. He is a good Muslim, and he will protect me and support me. We are meant to be together. He is the man I will spend my life with. I knew this to be the truth from the moment my mother introduced us. Together, we will work through this. Please understand, this is the best thing for me."

"Right, right," Molly said, rocking back and forth on the couch. "Fifteen is not legal in this state, I believe you need to be eighteen to marry... and you met him, what, two days ago? Please give my common sense some respect here."

"It's not a legal marriage, it is more like an engagement. We can be married when I turn seventeen, with guardian consent earlier in special circumstances."

Molly raised her eyebrows. "And you know this how?"

"After my mother introduced us, I did some research in the library. In Iran, the legal age for marriage is thirteen, according to Islamic law. And we both prefer Islam as our guide," said Emma. "I haven't asked Hamid about the sighe, but when I do, I am sure he will agree."

"But look, Emma, this is America, not Iran. Your infatuation with Hamid sounds like a high school crush—and what else could it be, at this point? You need to understand that I am looking out for your best interests. Two teenagers can't just shack up together. What would you do for money?"

"I will get a job while he is still in school. We will find a way."

"What about your own schooling? We need to enroll you in high school. We wanted to give you as much time with your mother as possible, but we can't put it off any longer."

Emma smiled. "I should have told you—I passed my GED two months ago. I already have a high school diploma."

Molly just looked at her, shaking her head. Then she stood and walked to the window, looking out at the soaking wet garden. Raindrops ran down the glass. She stood there for what seemed like minutes just staring out the window.

She then turned to Emma with a stern look said, "I need to think about this. Stay with us this week and let us meet Hamid, talk to him more. I hardly saw him at the funeral. I will agree to be open-minded, but you must agree to be open-minded as well."

Emma smiled, walked over and hugged her, "Thank you Molly. I agree."

CHAPTER NINE

The Imam sat waiting for Hamid to arrive. He had never been quite this nervous. If he was in Iran, he would still be in training. He was the Imam here because he was the only candidate with any training, and people seemed to like the way he led the prayers. Apparently, now he had been assigned the role of asking Hamid to marry Emma, and he had no idea how he had been backed into this corner. He hadn't realized his dilemma until Emma left and he started thinking about it.

He had a mentor in Iran that he could call upon, but it was difficult to contact him even when the country wasn't in chaos—now, there was no chance. He had been consulting every book he could think of for guidance, and he was sure the Koran would not say anything about a woman making a proposal to a man through her Imam. He could only hope that he wouldn't be committing some unforgivable sin.

In the end, he decided that a love of Allah, and a love of each other, and a mutual understanding and respect would have to be the couple's guiding principles.

A knock on his door snapped him out of his thoughts.

"Come in," said the Imam in english.

Hamid entered and greeted the Imam with a 'salaam', kneeling and bowing deeply. Given the circumstances, this display of devotion felt like a bit much. "Yes yes, thank you for that, now please have a seat," the Imam said uncomfortably.

Hamid rose and took a seat across from the Imam.

Shifting to Persian, the Imam asked "You are the friend of Emma, yes?"

Hamid responded in the same language. "Yes, Imam, we are friends just two days, but we have been through much together."

The Imam hadn't realized they'd known each other only two days. The information felt like a body punch. Now he had no idea what to do. What came out of his mouth was "Two days? Well you can sometimes learn much about a person in a short time."

There was an awkward silence, then Hamid finally said, "You asked to speak with me, Imam?"

"Yes yes. The woman, Emma. Are you fond of her, do you respect her?" asked the Imam.

"Yes Imam, she is a very strong woman. I have much respect for her; she has been through much and she is still very strong."

"Yes yes, I have noticed that as well, and I think many in our mosque were impressed with her yesterday," said the Imam.

"I think she has much to offer, and will be a good wife someday to someone, if he is a strong man," Hamid said. He caught the Imam's eye and they both chuckled.

"Well then, I hope you are a strong man," said the Imam, still chuckling. "Because she wants you to join her in a sighe."

Hamid blinked. He opened his mouth but no words came out.

The Imam watched him for a moment. "Perhaps you should speak with her. If the two of you come back together in agreement, I have decided I will prepare the proper paperwork, and you will be able to enter into a temporary marriage. You will not be able to have sex until she is of legal age and you decide to be permanently married, but you will be able to live together with my blessing and the blessing of Allah. You will need to get her guardian to agree as well, because of her age."

Hamid still sat there with a stunned look, staring at the Imam. After a few moments he said, "Thank you, Imam, I will speak with her. I am glad to know that she has already spoken with you. I would never have been able to ask her myself." With a goofy, confused smile he said, "there has never been a greater gift in the world than hearing your words. I am forever indebted." Hamid rose, bowed, and left the room.

As the door shut behind him, the Imam smiled and silently thanked Allah for his guidance. A chill ran through his body that he had never felt before. For some reason, he knew that Allah had chosen him to bring these two people together.

CHAPTER TEN

After weeks of dinners at home and outings with Emma and Hamid, Molly reluctantly agreed to the sighe. Emma assured her that she would return if anything went wrong. After the sighe was set up for the new couple and the guardianship worked out, Emma set about planning the next step.

Staying at the dorms with Hamid was not possible, so they decided that they must find an off-campus place to be together. Emma stayed with Molly while they searched. They found a small studio on a quiet street a mile from the school and close to a bus line. It had a long and narrow walkway, with a garden and a grassy area in the front. The unit that was available was at the very back, and was therefore set quite far back from the street. There was a small table off to the side, with a few outdoor chairs and an umbrella. Three or four other studio apartments fronted the length of the walkway in the one-story building. It seemed to be a good fit.

As Emma and Hamid followed the landlord to look at the available unit, Emma could feel stares from someone peeking out of one of the units. It had an American flag used as a window blind, and a small, dirty BBQ just outside its door. The other units had a few locked bikes outside their doors. In one unit, a collection of small white collectables sat on the window ledge.

The landlord seemed hesitant to show them the unit. "Are you married? Students?" he asked, as he opened the door.

"Yes, we are married. My mother has died and Hamid is going to school. I will be finding a job and we will be here for many years and not be any problem," Emma said, not explaining their sighe.

The man looked at her and nodded. "You just gotta understand that it is a difficult time. The embassy takeover in Iran has people on edge, I don't know how other tenants will react if I rent it to you."

Emma looked at him. In a low, firm voice she said, "I am an American citizen. My father is a diplomat and is being held as a hostage in the embassy you speak of. He is not one of the hostage takers."

The man looked stunned. "Holy shit." He thought for a moment, nodded, and then said, "The rent is $175 per month, all utilities included. There is a $200 deposit, first and last due upon signing."

They walked through the apartment, which required about a half dozen steps. A bed took up half the living space. A few feet from the foot of the bed was the kitchen space, which consisted of a hastily-put-together sink and a propane two-burner stove with a small propane tank underneath. A small refrigerator sat on the counter. There was no closet, but the bathroom had a nice, old-style claw foot tub with a shower curtain. Emma looked at Hamid and he shrugged, acknowledging to Emma that it would work.

"If we take care of the yard space, could you lower the rent to $150?"

The landlord looked at her, and looked at Hamid, eventually nodding. "OK, $150 per month, and you mow the lawn weekly and keep the place tidy, and put out the trash on Monday mornings."

"Agreed," said Emma. When the landlord stuck out his hand she did not shake it but looked to Hamid, who had been quiet throughout. He saw her look at him and understood, stepping forward to shake the man's hand.

The next day, Hamid and Emma set about preparing their new home, finding a desk and small dresser at the local thrift shop. Molly's husband Jim had a small truck and helped with the move. Jim was able to rig a rod next to the desk, that they could use to hang clothes.

As they were moving items in from the truck a shirtless man walked out of his apartment. He passed them in silence, went to his van and pulled out a long bag. He passed them again and returned to his apartment, loudly slamming the door behind him.

"Nice fellow," Jim said to Hamid as they continued carrying the desk into the apartment.

Emma overheard. "It will be fine," she said. "Once he knows us, I think he will be more comfortable."

Once settled in, Emma took control, cleaning and organizing the little space. Later in the evening when they were alone for the first time in their new home, they sat together at their tiny desk, and Emma pulled out a wallet from her satchel.

"This is what I have." She laid a wad of bills on the desk. "It is seven hundred and seventy dollars. I have been told that I will not have access to my mother's accounts, as I am a minor and my father is still alive. He cannot give me access either, as he is being held hostage. I do not know when I will have more money. The only reason I have this is because my mother had me hold the cash while we were traveling to Seattle. What is your situation with money?"

Hamid pulled out a checkbook and looked at the account balance. "I have around eighteen hundred dollars, after the check that we gave to the landlord man. I do not know when I will have more from my family, or if any of them are alive." He hesitated, choking on his words, then continued. "I can stay here on my student visa as long as I am in school, unless they change the rules."

Emma thought for a moment. "And what of your school costs? Do you have them paid?"

"I will have a tuition payment for next semester due next month. I was told the payments from the Iranian government programs for tuition have stopped. The tuition will be just over one thousand dollars, and there will be books to pay for as well."

Emma calculated the costs with a pad and pencil. She looked at the numbers for a moment. "I will need to find a job right away. Until things settle down and your family in Iran can help, we will have to figure things out ourselves. Actually, we need to assume that they will not be able to help, and that we are on our own. We must not spend any money other than for necessities, and then every penny must be accounted for."

Hamid was staring at her with a goofy grin. Annoyed, she looked at him. "What?"

He smiled at her, put his hand on hers, and in Persian said, "I know it has been a short time, my sweet love, but words cannot properly express my feelings for you. You are the love of my life. From the moment your mother introduced us, I knew this as truth. Blessed be to Allah for bringing us together."

Emma smiled shyly at him, then fell into his arms in silence.

CHAPTER ELEVEN

The next day Emma put on her favorite hijab and slipped into a dress that her mother had given her for her fifteenth birthday, while they were still in Iran. There was a restaurant called Afghan about five blocks away from their new home, and she decided she would go and speak with them about a job.

"They are probably Sunni, it could be difficult," said Hamid. He was referring to the problem of a thousand-year-old animosity between primarily Shia Iran and Sunni Afghanistan.

"I am applying to be a waitress, not an Imam. We are all Muslim."

"Yes," said Hamid. "I did not say impossible, but some Afghans do not like Iranians so much."

"Thank you for that. If he does not like other Iranians, I will make sure to highlight my American blood," she said, smiling at him.

"I should walk with you. It seems not so safe right now."

"I will be fine, thank you, sweet man. I think it would be better to go alone. I know this is hard, but at times in this country I must act more like an American or it makes things worse. Getting a job is most important right now, and I must do whatever it takes to make that happen."

She reached for his hand and squeezed it lovingly, then turned and left. As she walked through the courtyard, the man with the American flag in his window was cooking meat on the grill outside of his door. He looked disheveled—shirtless, with ragged jeans.

He watched Emma approach. As she passed him, under his breath he mumbled, "fucking camel jockey."

She continued down the walkway and turned quickly onto the sidewalk leading toward the restaurant. A sudden feeling of dread came over her—would he do some harm to Hamid? After a few blocks her heart settled down, and she started thinking more about the restaurant.

She had never had a job before, nor even applied for one, and had no idea what to expect. She walked in and saw a scattering of people at various tables, a lone waiter taking an order, and an older man doing bookwork behind the cash register. In the kitchen, a couple of women and a man were cooking and doing dishes.

The interior was decorated with mostly black-and-white photographs of what appeared to be Middle Eastern scenes. Men in turbans sat in a semi-circle on a hillside overlooking a valley, working with what appeared to be some sort of cheese. Three men sat proudly next to a gaudy safe, with huge stacks of bills in front of them. In another photo, a young boy was surrounded by twenty or so seated men. He appeared to be giving advice to a man in front of him, and every one of the men in the audience was staring at the boy.

Emma was examining this picture with fascination when the cashier approached from behind. "He is a *Tawis newis*, a fortune teller," said the man in Persian.

Emma looked at him and then back at the picture. She responded in Persian. "But he is so young, and yet he gains the respect of men much older."

"Ah yes," said the man. "But this is what makes this boy so special: he has a wisdom beyond his years. It is the sign of a great teacher and leader. Can I help you?" he said, shifting to English. "What brings you in here today?"

Emma looked at him directly. "I am looking for a job. I live near here and have noticed your restaurant is quite popular. Perhaps you are in need of someone?"

The man studied Emma a moment. "Perhaps. You look very young, though. What is your name and where are you from?"

Emma thought, then said strongly, "I am Emma of Iran, I am fifteen, and as your photograph illustrates, age is not that important. It is the heart and wisdom of the person that counts."

The man chuckled. "Nice to meet you, Emma of Iran. I am Asad of Afghanistan." He smiled broadly at her and then became serious. "It is a difficult time with the Iran problem. I would worry that people might be offended if you say you are from Iran."

Emma responded without hesitation. "They don't seem to be offended that you are from Afghanistan. Sometimes I think most Americans think the two are the same country."

Asad nodded. "Yes, sometimes there is not a lot of understanding of our region and peoples. I do not understand Americans at times either. Before the hostage crisis, my business was very slow, now it is very good. I need more help. I think perhaps an Iranian waitress would not be a bad thing. We will do some paperwork, then we will train you, Emma of Iran. We will have to find out how many hours you can work, due to your age. You can start tonight; please come back by four p.m."

"Thank you," she said with a subtle bow, her hand over her heart.

On her way home, as she turned from the sidewalk to their walkway, she was relieved that the disheveled man was no longer there.

"How did it go?" Hamid asked as she entered their apartment.

"Well I start at four p.m., so I think it went well," she said, smiling broadly. Turning serious, she added, "The man with the American flag called me a camel jockey as I walked by earlier."

Hamid looked baffled. "I do not understand, you do not ride camels. Why would he call you this?"

Emma suppressed her smile and said, "It is an insult, meant to be mean. He is very good at being mean. Perhaps we should contact the landlord."

"I do not know if it will help," replied Hamid. "There are many people like him here; his view is perhaps more normal than we know."

Emma nodded. "I think for every bad person like him, there are a thousand good ones. I think maybe we should just look for the good ones and ignore the bad ones."

"Yes," said Hamid. "But the bad ones are hard to ignore when they live next door. I think even other Americans would fear this man. I do not think his anger is just toward us—I think he is angry at the world."

Emma and Hamid soon fell into a routine that worked for both of them, doing their best to avoid their neighbor. Emma was able to get a special exception to work extra hours, due to her GED. She was making surprisingly good tips at the restaurant. She could never predict a good tipping table. At times there would be tables that would say rude things, then leave very large tips, as if they were trying to make up for their actions. Perhaps they realized their stupidity, and didn't know how to say it, so by opening their wallet they were relieved of their guilt.

She learned to respond to repetitive questions, like, "Why do you wear something that shows how repressed you are?" Her answer, "I wear it by choice, you should see what I make my husband wear!" was always sure to garner a laugh. Or "How can you be in a religion that is so hard on women?" She would respond with, "The religion isn't that hard on women, it is how it is interpreted that can be hard," a response that often confused the person enough that they didn't ask any more questions.

"Perhaps we should invite the neighbor to a picnic at the side table," Emma said to Hamid one day. "Maybe if he got to know us it might be easier."

Hamid stared at her in surprise, then shrugged, acknowledging with nod that he would be willing to try.

CHAPTER TWELVE

Jared didn't know how to react to the note under his door. He knew it came from the camel jockeys next door, but he was hammered drunk and stoned, and the note made no sense.

He set the note on the cluttered coffee table, stood from his wretched couch and went to the fridge for a beer, starting into his second six-pack of the day. He made it a point to keep it under a six-pack before noon—that way he knew that he was still in control, and that the alcohol didn't have a hold of him. Although it didn't really matter if it did. No one was going to tell him what to do, especially not his ex-wife, who wouldn't stop bitching at him about alcohol when they were married. Now she was with some rich computer guy. She couldn't possibly be happy, he was sure.

As he obsessively flipped back and forth among the four channels he could get on his TV, he fumed at all of the injustice around him. Showing up late and smelling of alcohol should not be a reason to get fired, not if his work was getting done. Sure, he wasn't always perfect with his welding, but who was? It was all a conspiracy against the white men of America; the country was going to hell.

Now he had a couple of camel jockeys living right next to him, thinking they were just as good as him?

He looked again at the note inviting him to a late-afternoon picnic at the table in back. He couldn't help but laugh out loud at the absurdity of it. Like he was going to be seen with a couple of terrorists? They really had a lot of nerve; they probably planned to poison his food. He just couldn't come up with a good reason why they would want to eat with him.

Maybe they thought he had secret information, and were trying to trick him into revealing something. He could just eat some food then leave. He wouldn't give them any information or American secrets that they could take advantage of, even if he knew any.

But what if the CIA was after them, and he was secretly filmed with them? He could be labeled as a terrorist sympathizer and would never again be able to go out in public.

Living next to people who obviously were not true Americans was something he'd never imagined himself doing. Maybe if he met them he could make his point, and they would understand why Americans were so much better than the rest of the world.

He turned on the radio to his favorite talk radio host, and tuned into the flow of the conversation, which exactly confirmed his thoughts: "They take our jobs, corrupt our Christian children, then want to blow us up!" a voice screamed from the radio. "This is America today: we are being invaded by the Middle East and we don't even know it!"

Jared got up and started pacing back and forth as he listened, becoming angrier and angrier. "The point here, folks, is that we have to stand up for what it means to be an American, and you all know what I mean. We need to keep these people out, and kick out the ones that are here. American jobs need to go to A-MER-I-CANS, it just isn't that complicated."

Jared continued pacing aggressively, agreeing to the words spewing from the radio. He crushed the empty can and grabbed another from the fridge as the radio voice continued. "Let me put it another way. If you're out of work and a true American, whose fault is that? If all this cheap labor wasn't coming from everywhere, wouldn't you still have that decent-paying job that you had before? Why do our politicians not understand this? Americans have a right to be FIRST—you don't get to come here and get ahead of us. That's the way it works. Americans need to WAKE UP and stop all these foreigners, especially the Arabs and Muslims. You all know what's happening in Iran; did I not predict this? The lefty liberals have taken over! It is time to RISE UP, and take back what is rightfully ours!"

Jared chugged the rest of the beer, crushed the can in his hand and went to the fridge for another. When he returned to the couch he reached down and pulled out his meth box. He had a few hits left, and he needed to be at the top of his game to deal with these people.

He was just the thankful for his guns, so he could protect himself and other Americans. With the Arabs moving in next door, he knew the invasion had begun. It was up to him to stop it and stop them. No one else here could see what was happening.

Maybe he could just beat the crap out of the guy, teach them a good lesson. He probably beats the crap out of his wife to make her dress like that, anyway. That's it! he thought. The husband is the real enemy. He had it figured out now, and he would surely be a hero for taking out the Arab wife-beater.

When the time came for the afternoon lunch he took his last hit of meth, grinning as the euphoric rush hit his brain. He checked his snub-nose revolver, loading and reloading it. He put it into his ankle holster and tucked his pants over it, making sure there were no bulges. He was ready.

CHAPTER THIRTEEN

Emma wiped her hands nervously on her dress as the man walked toward them. He looked even more disheveled than usual. She stepped forward. "Um, Hello. I am Emma, and this is Hamid."

The man grunted, "I'm Jared." Scowling, he slammed his six-pack on the table, peeled off a beer, cracked it open and sat down. Hamid sat nervously across the table from him. Emma put out some plates, smiling but already regretting the decision to ask the man to eat with them.

Jared sat, rocking slightly back and forth, staring directly at Hamid with hollow eyes. He picked up his beer and drank the entire thing in several large gulps, then slammed the empty can down on the table.

"You people are nothing but terrorists, and you want me to fucking eat with you. You want me to fucking eat with you. Well FUCK YOU!" Suddenly he rose to his feet and flipped the table up, tossing it up and out of the way. Plates, cups and food flew everywhere. Emma staggered backward and stood staring at him, frozen in shock. Hamid was glued to his chair, his hands up in a surrender gesture. Then the crazed man attacked.

"I'm gonna teach you fucking foreigners!" He lunged at Hamid, driving him off the chair and punching him to the ground.

"Stop it!" Emma screamed. She jumped on his back, but was no match for the burly American. He flung the tiny girl off him and continued to punch Hamid over and over, his scarred knuckles driving into the younger man's face.

Emma scrambled onto his back again, wailing and punching him, trying to hold his arms.

Jared turned and grabbed Emma and threw her across the grass. He then turned back to the defenseless and limp Hamid, continuing to punch with insane fury.

By then, Emma was back on her feet. She dove between the two, using her body to protect Hamid, the man wildly punching around her.

"Stop it, dude!" a voice exclaimed. Suddenly, Jared felt strong hands on his arms, dragging him off Hamid. Whoever had hold of him pulled him stumbling backward. He turned and attacked his assailant, reaching for his ankle holster.

Emma looked toward the wrestling men, the back of the unknown man toward her. Jared now had a gun in his hand and was pointing it at the man's face, only feet away. She buried her head next to Hamid's and covered her ears with her hands.

"Don't shoot me, man!" she heard, then a gunshot and a scream of shock. She didn't look up; she knew they were next. She snuggled closer to Hamid, her face pressed next to his, waiting for the shot in the back of her head.

Emma fell into a dream state, prepared for her own death. She felt her mother's hand, saw her face. Yasmin was smiling. "It will be alright," said her mother, and a sense of calm came over Emma, as she waited for the crazed man to shoot her.

She could not remember the prayer that she was supposed to say prior to her own death; she could only hope that Allah would be forgiving. She remembered the prayer she had said upon her mother's death, and began whispering it into Hamid's ear. "O Allah, forgive Hamid and me and elevate our station among those who are guided. Send us along the path of those who have come before, and forgive us, O lord of the worlds. Enlarge our graves and shed light upon us."

Comforted that she and Hamid would be dying together, she held him, her heart shifting from fear to acceptance. She waited in a trance, lying there with Hamid, face down, like she was floating, expecting the inevitable. She hoped it would be painless.

She waited a long time. Then she heard sirens approaching. The noise brought her out and back to reality. She then lifted her head and turned toward the grassy area. Jared was lying face up and motionless, fifteen feet from where she and Hamid lay.

CHAPTER FOURTEEN

"He should stay here for a few days just as a precaution, but he should be fine once the swelling subsides. His brain scans were all clear," said the doctor to Emma after he examined Hamid. Hamid's eyes were both swollen shut, but he was able to talk and sip fluids, his memory of the attack limited.

"We cannot afford the hospital, we do not have insurance. I will need to take him home with me," said Emma.

The doctor examined her face, his eyes kind. "Let me see what I can do," he said. "He needs to stay here."

After a few minutes the doctor returned and said "You will not have to pay. Check with the billing department down the hall and they will take care of everything."

Emma looked at him, unsure how to respond. "I do not understand," she said, "I thought everyone had to pay. It is the way it works, here in America."

The doctor chuckled and said, "Usually that is the case, but the phone has been ringing off the hook since the news story came out. There are more than enough people willing to cover your costs."

Emma blinked at him. "Are these people Muslim?"

The doctor gave her an odd look. "Well, I- I don't know, they are just random people wanting to pay the bill."

"If they are not Muslim, we cannot accept, as we do not know how the money was obtained," Emma said firmly.

The doctor looked at her quizzically. "What?"

"We cannot accept," repeated Emma. "Please, is he well enough to leave?"

The doctor was dumbfounded. "I-I-I do not want to release him yet. No, he is not well enough to leave."

"Then perhaps we can arrange payments, I have seven hundred dollars that I can give you today, and we can pay more as we have it."

The doctor shrugged. "Look, you'll have to check with the billing department, but I'm sure you can work something out. I will check back tomorrow. If his condition improves, I will allow him to be released, but only if he is better."

"Thank you doctor," said Emma, and she went back to sit with Hamid.

The next morning the Imam showed up and greeted Emma, shaking his head gently as he patted Hamid's arm.

"Let us give thanks to Allah that Hamid and you are still alive. The word of this has spread in the mosque, we are gathering a fund to cover your hospital costs," said the Imam.

Tears streamed down Emma's face. "Thank you, please pass along my gratitude to all at the mosque. I too am grateful for Allah's mercy. There was also a random American that saved us, he pulled the crazed man off of us, then I do not know what happened."

"Allah works in mysterious ways, it is a blessing to be under his grace."

Hamid moved his head towards the Imam, and was able to partially open one of his eyes, and he gave the Imam a slight smile. After the Imam left, the doctor came by and reluctantly signed the release order, giving Emma a long list of things to watch for. They rented a wheelchair and got on the bus to head home. When they arrived at their apartment, flowers and gifts surrounded their door. A woman who lived in a nearby unit but had not spoken with them other than a passing 'hello,' opened her door as Emma wheeled Hamid to their home.

The woman looked at Hamid, stifling a gasp with her hand when she saw his deformed and swollen face, then looked at Emma. "This was shocking for all of us, I just want you to know that it was not just an attack on you guys, but it was an attack on everyone. It was so shocking. I am so sorry this happened. Please let me help however I can."

Emma smiled at the woman. "Thank you, I appreciate your words. I think we will be fine, but if I need help I will ask. Perhaps you could open the door for me?"

The woman sprung into action, clearing a path through the flowers and using Emma's key to open the door.

As they were moving inside, the landlord arrived. He said, "I just want you to know that I had no idea the guy was as dangerous as he was or he wouldn't have been here. I just didn't know. I will be doing background checks on everyone going forward. I can tell you now that the people here now are all good people."

Emma acknowledged him with a small smile. "I do not hold you responsible. Each person must act out of their own belief, out of their own vision. He was a troubled man. Perhaps he could have gotten help if the circumstances were different, but I think he was just confused."

"And Hamid, will he be OK?" asked the landlord.

"The doctor said it will be a few weeks before the swelling and bruising subside, but the brain scans and tests were clear. He should be fine. I'm sure he will be asking for his books soon."

The landlord was visibly relieved. "That is a great relief. Please let me know if I can do anything, and if you have any issue again with anyone, I need to hear it as soon as it happens, and I will get involved personally."

Emma thanked both of them and shut the door, anxious to be alone to care for Hamid. She bent down next to the wheelchair so he could put his arm over her shoulder, and together they stood and awkwardly worked their way to the side of the bed. He sat and Emma lifted his legs onto the bed and fluffed the pillows behind him as he settled in, acknowledging to her that he was comfortable.

"I cannot see well, but would you read a chapter of my physics to me?" he asked slowly. "I do not want to fall behind, I do not know when I will be able to get back to class." He motioned to the textbook on his desk.

Emma smiled and went to make some chamomile tea. When it was ready she handed Hamid a biscuit and helped him bring the teacup to his mouth, then set the tea on the desk. She then grabbed the book from the desk and pulled up a chair.

"Chapter four, kinematics," said Emma.

Hamid smiled a painful smile, knowing the pronunciation wasn't quite right, but having a tea and a biscuit and his Emma reading physics to him was awfully nice considering what they had been through. Emma read for a while, but found it tiring because she didn't understand the concepts.

As she took a break from the reading to give him another sip of tea, she asked, "Why do you have interest in this? It is all so complicated."

He motioned for another sip of tea, then said, "Most of the medical students would agree with you, and take physics only because it is required, but to me, to me it is learning about God."

"What do you mean?" asked Emma, confused.

"Well, it is like this. Kinematics is one example, one study of motion. It explains things in mathematical terms, like why things move as they do. Machines, planets, atoms, everything. It is an explanation of how God created things. To understand kinematics is to understand one more thing about God. When I fully see it in my mind, I am closer to God."

Emma sat there staring at the book, absorbing his words. After a few moments, she looked at him and said "I want to be a doctor."

Hamid smiled at her with his swollen face. "And you will be a great one, I'm sure God will be pleased. It is good, actually, because I have been thinking about switching to nuclear engineering. You can be the doctor of the family and I will be the engineer." He smiled awkwardly.

Two days later Hamid's other eye opened and he was able to get in and out of bed without help, and Emma was able to go back to work.

"You have the number of the restaurant, call me if anything happens. They will let me leave if you need any help. I will bring some food home later, sweet man." She smiled and kissed him lightly on the cheek. He grimaced, faking pain. "You are bad," she said, smiling as she left.

CHAPTER FIFTEEN

Confused, the Dean of Medicine stared at the application of the young woman he was about to meet.

He pressed the button on his intercom and said, "Ms. Johnson, can you come in here a moment?"

When his secretary was standing in front of his desk, he said, "I don't understand. This applicant is sixteen years old, has very little in the form of transcripts, and has a GED instead of a high school diploma. What am I missing here? And why is she coming to me, and not to admissions?"

The woman shuffled her feet, obviously uncomfortable. "Well, sir, she is very persistent. Her score on the SAT was almost perfect. She is a waitress at a restaurant in Wallingford that I go to often. She was denied by admissions—her application did not even make it to an interview. But I think you should meet her. You did ask for more special-situation students in that memo last week."

The dean lifted his eyes, looking up at her without moving his head. Then he sighed loudly and nodded. He trusted Ms. Johnson's instincts. "Show her in when she arrives. She gets ten minutes."

Ms. Johnson smiled broadly. "Thank you, sir." She closed the door behind her as she left his office.

A few minutes later, Emma followed Ms. Johnson into the dean's unimpressive office. It was a simple rectangular room the with a huge, solid desk taking up most of the room's width. It looked like one would need to shuffle sideways to get behind it. To the left was a full-wall bookcase, meticulously organized.

"Hello," said the dean, rising from behind his desk. He wore a jacket and tie that seemed a bit casual, and was a handsome man with a gentle smile, with a full head of graying hair, neatly combed. "Please sit down," he said, gesturing to the chair across the desk from him. "Ms. Nicholson, is that correct?" Emma had used her father's surname on the application, as required.

"I prefer to use Aroundami, the name of my husband," she said as they both took a seat.

The dean looked again at the application. Wasn't she sixteen? "You are married?"

"In a way, yes. It is temporary marriage, like an engagement, but more. It is an Islamic tradition primarily used in Iran, called a sighe. Given our situations, it has been the right thing to do."

He put the application down and leaned back, eyeing her appraisingly. "Tell me more about your situation."

She sat up straighter. "What would you like to know about me?"

"Well, students accepted into our program have extensive academic and social records, usually at the top of their class. What makes you uniquely qualified, other than a good SAT score?"

She pursed her lips, looking a bit irritated, then looked him directly in the eyes. "I know two of the questions I missed on the SAT. They were so absurdly biased that I refused to answer the way they wanted."

The dean chuckled.

Emma paused a moment. "I speak three languages fluently: English, French and Persian. I also speak some German and

Dutch. My father is a diplomat, so we have traveled and lived in many beautiful places in the world—the last one being Iran, where he is now being held hostage, unfortunately. My mother died three months ago of breast cancer."

She stopped to gather herself, regaining her composure. "I wish that we could have spent more time in Iran. I loved it, but now I fear I may never be able to go back. My mother home-schooled me. She was a very good teacher, and there were also many brilliant interns along the way that helped with my studies."

The dean smiled at the lovely woman in front of him. For some reason, her story resonated with him. "Why is becoming a doctor important to you?"

She thought a moment. "My husband explained it to me best. He said that to understand life, to become educated and to learn how the world works, is to know God. If you believe in God, what better service can you do than to educate yourself on how to fix his greatest creation, which is us? My mother's passing also was a moment when I recognized that I wanted to be a healer, that I wanted to be able to help however I could to relieve people's pain and suffering. I have seen much suffering and poverty in my travels and life abroad, and I want to do something to change that."

The dean studied Emma, thinking. After a few moments he stood. "Thank you for coming in today. I have a staff meeting shortly and need to get prepared; my apologies for the brevity of our meeting. I will speak with admissions and see if we can get a meeting arranged. Ms. Johnson will set that up and contact you in a few days."

CHAPTER SIXTEEN

It had been weeks since her meeting with the admissions department. She had resigned herself to working and helping Hamid however she could with his studies, and letting God decide her direction.

When she returned one day from her restaurant shift, a letter was waiting for her in the mailbox. It was addressed to her from the Admissions Department the University of Washington.

She laid the envelope next to her on the bed and stood to make a cup of tea. It would either be a yes or no, she reminded herself. If it was no, she still had Hamid and God. If it was yes, she still had Hamid and God. Either option was acceptable.

Her rationale didn't make it any easier to open the envelope. She sat back down on the bed with her tea in hand and looked at it again. She picked up the envelope and held it to the light, but was unable to pick up any hints, and laid it on the bed next to her again.

She continued to sit, sipping her tea, but unable to open the envelope. Maybe her blood sugar was low. She stood and went to the counter and took out a tea biscuit, making sure it was one of the honey options. She sat back down as she silently ate her biscuit and sipped her tea, not looking at the envelope.

After what felt like an eternity she heard Hamid come home. He entered the room and looked at Emma. "What is wrong?"

She stood and lunged for him, her cup dropping to the floor with a crash. She wrapped herself around him, unable to explain. As he held her, he saw the envelope on the bed. He softened his hold on her and reached for the envelope, comprehending the moment.

Emma let go of him and moved to the bathroom to get the broom. Hamid studied the envelope and watched Emma obsessively clean up the broken teacup.

"It will be all right," he said, as she finished tidying up the mess. He reached for her hand and they sat down on the bed together. He turned the envelope over and carefully opened it, pulling out the letter as she buried her head in his shoulder.

"It says, Dear Mrs. Aroundami, Congratulations, you have been accepted into the University of Washington's School of Medicine."

CHAPTER SEVENTEEN

In January the new quarter started, and Emma and Hamid began their new routines. Studies went well; both were excelling in their classes. Their worlds were primarily focused around each other. They had planned classes so that they could meet on breaks, walk together, have lunch together—whatever they could do to coordinate as much time together as possible.

It was President Elect Reagan's Inauguration Day, and the campus seemed to be alive. They walked together on their usual route to the student union, picking up conversations about the hostages, but it was unclear what was happening. As they walked into the student union, they looked up at the TV, surrounded by students.

"Once again, the hostage crisis is over. It has been confirmed. The American hostages are all now on a plane headed back to the US," said the newscaster.

Emma absorbed the news, then turned to Hamid. "I will call Molly. Perhaps she and Jim could help us get my father settled in somewhere. Our home is too small for three."

"He can stay with us until things are figured out," said Molly on the phone with Emma. "He can stay in the small unit downstairs that we keep for family. Do you know his condition?"

"No, I have very little information. I received a call from the State Department a few minutes ago saying he would be arriving at SeaTac at seven o'clock tonight."

"Typical government," said Molly. "Let us pick you up, we can go together. I'm not sure how to put this, but it might be best if Hamid doesn't go, initially."

Emma thought for a moment. "I think you may be right. I will be waiting for you. Thank you, Molly, for all your help."

At the airport, as they waited at the gate for Eric, Emma was growing increasingly nervous, not sure what to expect. When all of the people had apparently exited the plane and Eric had not appeared, she and Molly looked at each other, not knowing what to do. Molly went to the podium just as an airport attendant hurried past them, pushing an empty wheelchair down the ramp. Molly said to the woman at the counter, "We are waiting for Eric Nicholson. He is supposed to be on this plane."

"Yes, he will be out shortly, apparently he is ill. Please give us a moment." Shortly afterward, the woman pushing the wheelchair reappeared. The man in the wheelchair was gaunt and haggard. He smiled bravely when he caught sight of Emma.

"Hello, sweet child," he said, reaching for her hand as she bent down to give him a gentle hug. "They wanted to keep me for observation and I just wanted to get here. In hindsight, I probably should have stayed in DC a few days. This last stretch has been difficult." He turned to Molly. "Hello, my dear. Thank you for looking after my girl."

Emma took over pushing the wheelchair. She bent to his ear and said softly, "As your new doctor and caretaker, I am now prescribing a hospital visit. We will admit you for a few days to have you evaluated, and I do not want to hear any complaint about it."

Eric could do nothing but smile. She reminded him of Yasmin so much that it was eerie. "Yes, Mother. I will do as you say."

CHAPTER EIGHTEEN

The doctor walked in and looked at the new patient's chart. "I'm a little confused here. Are you getting treatment? Who is your primary doctor?" He continued to flip through the pages of blood tests. Eric and Emma looked at each other. Emma took the lead.

"This is my father, Eric Nicholson. He was just released from Iran. He was one of the hostages."

The doctor looked stunned, then turned his focus one hundred percent to Eric. "I did not know this, my apologies." He probed Eric's chest and abdomen with his stethoscope, tapping in different locations while moving the instrument around. "Pain level? Location of pain? Other symptoms?" he asked.

"Taking a leak is a nightmare; it just doesn't seem to flow as much as it should. My whole body aches, especially my right hip."

The doctor continued checking and tapping, not looking up. "How long has this been going on?"

Eric shrugged. "I had an appointment to see the doctor before the embassy was taken over. So, over a year.

The doctor straightened and glanced at Emma, then turned back to Eric. "I need to do a biopsy on your prostate. We also have a new machine called a CT scanner. It takes a while, but it will give us a good picture of your bones. I'm going to move you to the front of the line and get you in today. It will be challenging—they are not fun machines to be lying in—but we need the image. I'll also increase your pain medication, if needed."

Emma went to Eric as the doctor left the room and put her hand on his. "It could be many things," she said, trying to sound reassuring.

"Including prostate cancer, I'm guessing," he said stoically.

"It is one of the possibilities, yes." Emma's eyes were filling, and she struggled to get the words out.

Eric sighed and looked out the window at the giant evergreen tree next to the building. "Well, it is what it is. I was sure I was going to die many times in that damn embassy. If I end up dying of this, at least I made it out of that hell hole."

He took a deep breath and turned from the tree to Emma. "I understand you have been living with a guy."

Emma met his eyes, nervously shifting in her seat. "Yes, his name is Hamid. We did not know the right way to tell you."

"Well, I can appreciate that. I was held captive by some pretty angry Iranian men. When held for so long with so much anger everywhere, you start to think that they all must be like this, but I know you would not be with such a man."

She put her hand on his arm and gently squeezed it. "Hamid is a wonderful man, father. I met him in the hospital just before mother died. She introduced us. I know that she felt in her heart how special Hamid was, even if her time with him was brief."

"I didn't know that," her father said. "I would like to meet your Hamid; he sounds like an interesting fellow. And you are right; your mother had very good instincts regarding people."

"I will bring him tomorrow when I come. We will be here in the late afternoon, after classes."

"Thank you, sweetie. It would be good to have you here when I get the news about my condition."

Emma smiled as she squeezed his hand. She stood and kissed him gently on the cheek. "I'm sure it will be fine. I will see you tomorrow."

The next day after classes, Emma and Hamid headed out for the one-mile walk to the hospital. The doctor had set an appointment time to discuss the results of the tests that a nurse had relayed to Emma. They walked quickly to get to the hospital on time, the brisk walk helping to offset the cold of the mid-winter day.

"Hello, Hamid," said Eric as they approached his bedside, reaching for a handshake, not waiting for an introduction.

"Hello, sir," Hamid said, gently shaking Eric's hand.

"Always use a firm handshake in America, Hamid, best advice I can ever give you."

Hamid smiled, then reached back for a second handshake.

"Ha! Much better," said Eric, chuckling.

"It is an honor to meet you, sir. I have heard endless stories about you," said Hamid, still holding Eric's hand.

The doctor entered the room, frowning at a folder in his hand. "Good morning, all. I have some test results that we need to go over. It probably should be family only."

Eric turned his look from the doctor to Emma and Hamid. "This is my family. Please proceed."

Emma and Hamid stood on the opposite sides of the bed as the doctor opened his folder again and hesitated. He looked up, making eye contact with Emma, Hamid and Eric in turn, then began.

"You have stage four prostate cancer. It has metastasized to your bones, as well as to other areas."

The room became silent for a moment as they all absorbed his words.

"Well, that does explain a few things," Eric said with a resigned tone. "Where do we go from here?"

The doctor hesitated, then took a deep breath and blew it out. "We might be able to slow it, but we cannot stop it. Treatment should have started a year ago. I suspect that you are in more pain than you're letting on."

"You adjust to pain," Eric said. "How much time do I have?"

The doctor shook his head. "Not long. Enjoy every day. I will do my best to keep your pain down. Be careful with your movements; your bones are very fragile. We could start radiation therapy, but I fear it is too late and would make your final days miserable. However, it could extend things a bit."

"Thank you. I appreciate your honesty," Eric said.

The doctor left the room as Emma and Hamid stood next to the bed. Tears streamed down Emma's face as she gently squeezed Eric's hand.

"Everything's going to be all right, sweetie," he said. "I see your mother's strength in you. I'm just sorry this has happened so soon in your life. But you know, your mother and I will always be watching over you."

Two weeks later, Eric died. He had requested that there be no funeral, and that his ashes be spread in the ocean near the San Juan Islands, a favorite spot of his. On a cold, rainy Sunday, Molly and Jim drove Emma and Hamid to the islands.

Emma carried Eric's ashes in a shoulder bag, constantly touching the urn with her hand. After the long ferry ride, the ship winding its way through the beautiful group of islands, they drove to a little vacant waterfront park a few miles from the ferry landing and parked the car. The rain had picked up in intensity.

"Give me just a moment," Emma said, exiting the car in the pouring rain and quickly walking down to the water's edge.

She pulled the urn out of her shoulder bag, opened it and tossed the contents as far as she could out into the water. She watched as the ashes slowly floated away, then ran back to the car.

As she got in, dripping wet, everyone was looking at her. She looked back at them and shrugged. "I think it is how he would want it. No tears or speeches, just get it done."

They all turned and looked for a moment again at the wind-ruffled sea where she had tossed the ashes.

"OK, then," Jim said. He started the car and they headed back to Seattle.

CHAPTER NINETEEN

Emma nervously walked into the building, with no idea what to expect. The business name 'In Chap's Defense' was kind of odd, but the ad she had seen made it clear that it was a self-defense school. She had done some research looking for one run by a woman, but there simply weren't any. It would be difficult to honor her beliefs while training around men, but she was determined. She peeked into the workout room and there was just a scattering of men sparring with each other.

"Can I help you?" came a powerful and frightening voice behind her.

She turned to see a man with a square jaw and chiseled face smiling at her. He could have been Middle Eastern himself, with dark eyes and a swarthy complexion. He looked very fit. "Yes, thank you," Emma said, shaken. "I am interested in being able to defend myself."

Her words inspired a bold laugh from the man. "Well, this is a first for me, a Persian woman walking into my establishment."

She blinked at him. "How did you know I'm Persian?"

"It was an educated guess. A Sunni Arab woman wouldn't set foot in here without her man present. Iranian women tend to be a little more independent," he said with a gentle smile. "You have come to the right place. I'm John Chapman, but everyone calls me Chap. I'm owner of this little show. And you are?"

"I am Emma, of Iran, and you are correct with your guess." She was impressed by his insight.

The man shifted into crude Persian. "So, Emma of Iran, do you want to learn to kill, or just disable your enemy?"

Emma laughed, and responded in Persian, "Perhaps to be so intimidating that I need to do neither."

"Good answer," Chap said, smiling. Shifting back to English, he said, "My experience is that having all options at your disposal is the best."

"How is it that you speak Persian?" asked Emma.

"I was special forces over there for a while," said Chap, "retired a few years back, so I'm still holding on to my Persian. In fact, I'll make a deal with you: you can do the training for half price if we do it all in Persian. I do want to hang on to that language."

Emma smiled and responded in Persian, "It is a deal."

She left with a good feeling about the man. It was not going to be too expensive, with the deal they had worked out, and he seemed interested in teaching her. Chap had given her a form to fill out and bring to the first class. She went home and pulled it out of her purse, then sat at the tiny desk in their apartment and thought about the attack in their yard, and how it would have been very hard to defend against. The man was just crazy and out of his head. How can you defend yourself against something like that; something you don't see coming?

She thought about the questions on the form. She did not want to learn about guns, it seemed to her that the less guns around, the better. When she heard of the arsenal the crazy man had set out on his bed, she realized that the country they were living in was a very dangerous place at times. In a way, she was thankful that it had all happened the way it had... Hamid had recovered, the man was dead, and no one else had gotten hurt. Perhaps if it had not happened as it did, he would have taken his guns and slaughtered a bunch of people. She shuddered at the thought.

The form asked for her training goals. Having some basic skills to fend off a man, someone trying to rape or otherwise harm her, would be good. Then she considered the section on knives. What if she were good at defending herself with a knife? She decided it would be the one lethal object that she would learn to use, and just hoped that she would never have to use it.

Emma arrived early for her first class and handed Chap her form. "Knives, huh?" said Chap, looking at her with a grin. "We've got a little time, let me show you the knife room." He deviously wiggled his eyebrows up and down, making Emma giggle.

The knife room was about ten feet wide and twenty feet long, with a board at the far end that had obviously been stuck a thousand times.

Chap took a knife from the arsenal and showed it to Emma. "This is a throwing knife. It is specially balanced, but sometimes a good heavy kitchen knife will work in a pinch." He flipped the knife over in his hand, then before Emma knew what was happening, turned and threw the knife at the board. It stuck chest high with a loud 'twang,' the knife still rattling in the board as he walked over and pulled it out.

"That was a full-rotation throw. Normally I don't teach that one so much—a three-quarter or half-rotation is much more practical in a pinch. You try," he said, handing her the knife.

She took it automatically, then looked at him, rolled her eyes, and started to hand the knife back to him.

He looked at her sternly. "Look, you've got a guy charging you from fifteen feet away, your babies are behind you, you have no chance if he reaches you with that club in his hand. You have got to throw that thing and not miss, or you and your babies will die."

He didn't actually get the word 'die' out. Emma turned and stepped into the throw with all her might and a fierce look on her face... the knife stuck with a 'twang' in the board, chest high, dead center.

Chap stared at the knife, then looked at Emma, then back at the board. "Yes, that was a good start," he said in English, forgetting that they were supposed to be speaking Persian.

Emma realized quickly that she had been very lucky with her first knife throw; it was the only one she was able to stick in the board the rest of the class. Time after time, week after week, the knife would fall harmlessly to the floor, most throws bouncing off the board as she practiced. The half-hour of the two-hour weekly classes dedicated to the knife room seemed to be going nowhere, and she was getting frustrated.

"You're aiming. I can almost see your brain analyzing it," Chap snapped one day in Persian. "Your form is perfect, but your heart is not in it." He grabbed the knife and flipped it a few times. Then he turned and screamed viciously as he threw the knife, sticking it in the board dead center, chest high.

"No more gentle practicing," he yelled at her, "I want you to scream as loud as you can every time you throw that fucking thing. No more bullshit!"

He stormed over to the board, grabbed the knife, and thrust it at her, screaming, "Kill that motherfucker!!"

Emma turned and screamed as loud as she could, throwing the knife in one vicious motion. It stuck dead center, chest high.

CHAPTER TWENTY

Eric's estate lawyer had set up the meeting. The office was on the fortieth floor—Emma was sure she had never been that high in a building before.

The lawyer rose to greet her, his blue eyes warm. "Hello, Emma, I'm Charles Aires. I don't think we have ever met but your father has told me a lot about you."

Once they were both seated, Mr. Aires started right in. "Well, there are a few things to discuss here. Fortunately your father was able to contact me prior to his passing. Otherwise, things would have been most difficult with both your mother and father passing away so prematurely." Then, realizing he was being insensitive, he added, "I'm very sorry this has all happened. I think your father was a great man. He was not just a client, but also a good friend."

"Thank you very much," said Emma. "Your words are greatly appreciated."

He smiled at her. "Let me just dive right in. Your father and mother have left you a lot of money, and there is likely more to come. It is set up in a trust. You will be getting ten percent of the trust each year until you are twenty-five, then the entire amount will be released." He handed her a check. She looked at the check, payable to her, in the amount of $32,367.00.

"If you have issues with the bank setting up an account because you are a minor, let me know and I can act as trustee." He smiled. "But you have complete control over the funds. Those were your father's specific wishes."

Emma was still looking at the check. She said slowly, "You are saying that my parents saved over 300,000 dollars?"

Charles nodded. "Well, yes. Between their retirement accounts and other bank accounts, it's more like $320,000. There could be some adjustments after tax time, but that number is pretty close. You might also be getting an additional lump sum payout from the State Department at some point, but that seems to be on hold for now. The Iranian government was promised immunity from lawsuits as a condition of releasing the hostages."

Emma thought for a moment. "It is enough. I do not want a lawsuit or other action regarding my father's captivity, and I do not believe that he would, either. It just happened, and the risk came with his job. He loved what he did."

Charles looked at her, appreciating the insight. "I understand. However, if there is a settlement offer, I will contact you and perhaps we could decide what to do then."

"That will be fine, thank you," said Emma as she stood. "Thank you for helping our family. I appreciate your professionalism." She gave him a nod of her head with her hand over her heart, then turned and left.

CHAPTER TWENTY-ONE

The next two years went by quickly. Emma and Hamid continued to live in their tiny little apartment while going to school, even after the unexpected inheritance. There was something about the simplicity of living small that helped them both with their studies. Emma decided to drop down to just one day a week at the restaurant, but wanted to continue working there as she had made many dear friends. She doubled her workload at school, however, and was quickly catching up to Hamid. She loved the clinic shifts and was becoming interested in women's health as her primary focus.

When she read about the staggering numbers of women in the developing world that have birthing complications due to the lack of trained doctors, she decided that this area would be her focus, and set her mind and course load in that direction.

On Emma's eighteenth birthday, she and Hamid decided to go for a walk in the Arboretum, which was a lovely inner-city garden of native trees and wildlife near the school. They walked hand in hand quietly, both appreciating the break from studies and solitude of the location.

"You seem to have something on your mind, sweet man," said Emma.

Hamid was always impressed by how well she could read him; it greatly helped him to express himself when she knew what he was going to say before he said it.

He stumbled a bit finding the words, then gained his composure. "You are eighteen now, and we have been in the sighe for over two years. I was thinking perhaps we should go to the Imam and ask that it be made permanent."

Emma could not help but smile. She stopped walking, turned, and enthusiastically hugged him. "Yes, yes, yes!" she said, overwhelming him with kisses.

Hamid gently stopped her. "Sometimes your American side can be overwhelming," he said, laughing playfully. He went back to holding her hand and they continued walking.

"Our situation is odd," said Hamid thoughtfully. "Normally in Iran our parents would arrange it, prepare the Khastegari ritual, we would be introduced, and it would all take much time. It would be a big family event. We are different with so many aspects, neither of us has family to help."

"I always dreamed of my own wedding," Emma murmured. "The rituals, the family connection, the foods, the gifts. The Iranian wedding is a beautiful thing." She thought for a moment. "Perhaps we could ask the Imam if there are people who might stand in as our relatives. We could contribute money so that it would not be a burden, and we could do it as a community."

Hamid looked at her, smiled and nodded, "that is a good idea, yes."

CHAPTER TWENTY-TWO

If the Imam had learned one thing, it was to be cautious when the young woman Emma approached with an idea. But once she stated her wishes and left, he thought her latest idea might work. He knew his flock, and knew they would all want to participate in the young couple's wedding. Many of them had taken Emma and Hamid under their wing from the start. After praying to Allah for guidance, he decided it was a good idea and agreed to allow it. He announced the plan shortly after afternoon prayers, which only a few men attended that day.

But when word got out, the lobbying for key positions began. Soon the entire mosque was abuzz with the prospect of participating in the marriage of Emma and Hamid. If in Iran the families would surely have control over the proceedings, in the mosque it was suddenly chaos.

The Imam made it clear that he would speak only to the men of the families who wanted to be involved. But the reality soon became apparent: the women were in control and the men were simply doing as they were told. The Imam quickly realized he had no idea what he had gotten himself into.

The backroom negotiations became as intense as a military war room. None of the men were happy about the sudden disruption in their daily routines, as their wives were paying more attention to the wedding planning than to taking care of things at home.

Unfortunately, the Imam's interactions with women, other than his own wife, were very limited.

The Imam and his wife had a much more sheltered and traditional marriage, and generally kept to themselves outside of the mosque. He had never given much thought to how people interacted with each other in their marriages behind closed doors. It seemed that when it came to American-Iranian women, they tended to have much more control over the dynamics of the family, even if it was behind the scenes.

By the third day he had given up trying to negotiate the escalating tensions. He isolated himself in his chamber, with a handwritten sign on his door saying, "No discussions today regarding the wedding, I am consulting Allah." This prevented even the most desperate husbands from seeking relief.

By the fourth day the disputing families had decided to vote on which families would be responsible for the different rituals, which led to another dispute about whether the women would be allowed to vote. When this was suggested by one of the older and more conservative men of the mosque, every man in the room groaned at his stupidity for suggesting it, which was confirmed by the sudden angry outburst by the women in the room. The motion was quickly voted down, and the man who had suggested it silently skulked out of the room.

The argument changed to how much the traditional aspects must be followed. The younger and more progressive side pointed out the fact that Emma was far from traditional, that she was working and at the top her class in the medical school. The side arguing for the more traditional wedding pointed out that Emma was one of the few women who consistently wore the hijab, and that Hamid's family was from a very conservative tribe in Iran. This itself led to an argument about tribal law and tradition that got completely off the point, and by the time late-afternoon prayers approached, no one was happy.

Finally the Imam stepped in, announcing that after the prayers he would make an announcement to everyone, including the women, which was a highly unusual event. Most of the men in the room were visibly relieved that their wives would be allowed to participate—the last few days of acting as intermediaries was wearing on everyone.

The Imam walked into the packed room with a paper in his hand. "After much prayer and asking Allah for guidance, this is how the wedding of Emma and Hamid will be handled." He realized too late that he should have said Hamid's name first.

He looked sheepishly around, but no one seemed to mind, so he continued. "For the next three days, starting tomorrow, Hamid shall stay with the family of Arshod, and Emma shall stay with the family of Marzban." Spontaneous gasps and murmurs of disgust could be heard.

The Imam waited until the room quieted, then continued. "The rest of you, over the next few evenings, should go to these families with the reasons why you think Hamid should accept Emma, and why Emma should accept Hamid. Should they both agree, the Baleh Boran ceremony will be held on the fourth night at the home of Armand."

The color started returning to Armand's face. After the announcement that they would not be hosting either Emma or Hamid during the Khastegari, he was in a panic over his wife's reaction. He dared not even look at her—he could only imagine the fury in her eyes. She was not used to not getting what she wanted. But being given the task of hosting the Baleh Boran ceremony, where the couple would be expressing their acceptance of the proposal, had brought back honor to his family. When he glanced at his wife he could see that she was already planning the most elaborate Baleh

Boran of the last sixteen centuries, even though it was normally a simple affair.

The Imam went on distributing the different ceremonies over the following week. "On the night following the Baleh Boran, the Namzadi will be held at the home of Massoud. The night after that, the Shirini Khoran shall be held at the home of Omid... " and on and on.

Each night there was to be a new party, each covering a different tradition. Some would normally have been held on the same night, but by spreading them out on consecutive nights the Imam was able to accommodate each family that was requesting a formal part in the wedding. Fortunately, traditional Iranian weddings had an endless number of steps both before and after the wedding, and so in the end, everyone was assigned an important part, and each was able to claim some honor. Not all were happy about the break from normal tradition, but as soon as the meeting was over they started planning the week, and their own part in the wedding of the century.

The plan was pure genius, and the Imam knew it. He also knew he could never have done it without Allah's help. When he returned to his quarters, he locked the door behind him, kneeled down on his favorite pillow, bowed deeply, and thanked Allah endlessly for his guidance. He had never felt as close to Allah as he did at that moment, having been shown the way to keep his flock together.

By the time the wedding day arrived a month later, Emma was sure she had gained ten pounds. The sweets and elaborate food from one party to the next were endless, with every family trying to out-do the next. The end result was spectacular spreads of old Iran that even the grandparents of the group thought were the best they had ever been a part of.

In their search for last-minute private facilities near Seattle, they had encountered much resistance when the venue operators learned it was an Iranian wedding. In the years following the hostage crisis there was a lot of prejudice and suspicion regarding Iranians living in the US. After much searching, they were able to find an old facility at a city-owned park in Everett, a town just north of Seattle that was, ironically, home to a military base. The facility had a last minute cancellation and so the mosque was able to book the venue.

The space in Everett was perfect. It was in a county park, set back in a large open area with giant evergreen trees everywhere. The building's main room was large, with several small rooms in the back and a commercial kitchen. The front of the room had a stage where the Sofreyeh Aghd—table of the wedding—was set up. It was a huge, seemingly-endless table holding spices, breads, fruits, and special dishes that each signified something special. Symbols of fertility, with eggs and nuts, were scattered throughout. An improvised burner was set up off to the side with a young man assigned to keep gently adding Frankincense and other spices to ward off evil and purify the ceremony. A golden bowl near the front was gradually being filled with gold and silver coins as the guests arrived, signifying prosperity. Simple breads, cheeses and greens, symbolizing the basic foods needed to sustain life, were placed strategically on the table. The dishes went on and on; nothing was missed. There were so many hands helping that it was a feast like no one had seen before. Each family brought some unique dish from their own tribe or region to add to the table.

The seats for the bride and groom were at the head of the table, with a large ornate mirror set up directly across from their seats, so that when the bride arrived and was seated with her face fully veiled, the first thing that Hamid would see when she took the veil off was the reflection of her beauty.

The room naturally segregated itself into an eclectic mix of tables. There was the niqab table, of fully veiled and face-covered women in their formal Islamic finest. All their husbands were at a table closer to the bride and groom's table. Then there was the Afghan table of Asad and his family, and other prominent Sunnis that Emma knew.

There was a table of young, single, American-born Iranian women, mostly college friends of Emma's, all dressed in tight-fitting and relatively revealing dresses, making the more traditional men in the room very uncomfortable. The young women were quietly discussing the potential availability of the amazing selection of dark and handsome men at the wedding feast.

It seemed that every family invited brought along a single man or woman, increasing the body count by forty or fifty more than expected. Extra tables were quickly set up toward the back for the overflow of guests. The tables were not as ornate as the pre-planned ones, but no one seemed to mind. It was a great honor to be present at the wedding of Emma and Hamid. For everyone present, the group effort of the mosque had turned it into the event of the year. There was no problem with food; the overwhelming number of dishes prepared by the different families would have fed twice the anticipated number of guests.

The band was up and playing as the guests arrived, the music drawing people into the room like a siren's song. The lead singer was a beautiful woman who went by the name of Shaniha. She was accompanied by four men, three playing mandolin-style guitars and the fourth drumming two animal-skin drums with his bare hands. The group was one of the more popular in Iran prior to the revolution. When music was one of the first things the new Islamic government banned, they were relegated to secret and somewhat dangerous gigs at private homes. Eventually, they had decided as a group to leave.

The group was able to arrange a special presentation in Turkey and simply didn't go back to Iran. The Turkish government was thrilled to have one of the finest music groups in the whole middle east. The new Islamic government in Iran basically ignored the defection, relieved that there was not a public fight over their blasphemous music. Fortunately for the wedding, there was a world music festival going on in Seattle the following weekend, and so the wedding was treated to the group.

The Imam was making the rounds, doing his best to greet everyone in the room. He worked his way around the room, greeting and blessing each table in his jovial and pleasant manner. As he approached the table of young women, his anxiety grew. He thought about what he was going to say and silently prayed to Allah for guidance. The Imam was open-minded, and was probably as liberal and westernized as any Imam in the Muslim world, but a table full of scantily dressed, beautiful young women was too much even for him.

As he approached the table, the whispering and giggling stopped, and ten sets of young, heavily made-up eyes were staring straight at him. There was a stony silence, and all of the other tables within earshot suddenly quieted.

What came out of the Imam's mouth was "May all of you blessed be Allah and to those he should want of wandering sheep." This, of course, made no sense to anyone. The young women continued to stare. The Imam thought for a moment, then bowed and hurried on to the next table, leaving the girls looking at each other, all completely perplexed.

Eventually everyone settled in and anxiously awaited the bride's entrance. Hamid was seated at the head table with the ornate mirror in front of him. It had been positioned and repositioned a dozen times to make sure that the bride's proper and perfect reflection be forever remembered in his eyes. Hamid's substitute father Arshod and his wife were seated to his right; Emma's Marzban and his wife were seated to the left of Emma's empty chair. Armand and his wife were also at the table, as much to keep the peace as to observe any specific tradition about inviting the hosts of the Baleh Boran. Molly and Eric were also invited to the main table at Emma's insistence, as well as the Imam and his wife.

When all were settled into their seats, Hamid caught the Imam's eye, indicating it was his turn on the stage. The Imam was still recovering from his now-infamous speech at the young womens' table, but he was able to refocus. As the gentle song wound down, he worked his way to the designated speaking area, and the room hushed. He nodded and secretly smiled at the band as he faced away from the crowded room, himself quite enjoying the lovely music. He had always appreciated the sounds of the mandolin.

He turned to witness a silent room of beauty. The faces, the colors, the smells and love in the room was something he was sure Allah himself would marvel at.

"Blessed be to Allah," the Imam began, "that we can all be here today to bear witness to a glorious joining of two very deserving people."

The Imam's heart was smiling so much that it worked its way to his face. He was simply glowing, and it rubbed off on the entire room—smiles were everywhere. Even Armand's wife let go of her thoughts for a moment and was entirely focused on the Imam, smiling and putting her hand on Armand's hand, much to his surprise.

"May the woman Emma now show herself, may Allah's presence grace this room and everyone in it, and lead Emma to her place next to her husband Hamid."

He nodded to the man in front of the door at the back of the room, and all eyes turned that way.

The door opened to the vision of a veiled beauty. Emma slowly walked from the darkened room behind her, out into the main room, and made her way gracefully along the path of Persian rugs laid out in anticipation of her beauty.

The silence and loving stares were interrupted only by the sounds of birds twittering in the trees outside. Emma's dress was a spectacular white and flowing satin, with subtle beads and tassels adorning the multiple layers. Her headdress was a softly layered hijab, with a loose veil hiding her features.

Her body was no longer that of a thin, petite teenage girl. In the last ten days it had transformed into the perfect vision of a Persian beauty, everyone in attendance would agree—especially the table of young women who were all instantly envious, and were now longingly looking around the room, each searching for her own husband-to-be.

Emma gently approached the head table with her face hidden. Hamid stood in front of it. He held out his hand palm up, and she laid her hand on his. Then he guided her to her seat. He helped her adjust her dress and snugged the seat comfortably forward, as all in the audience continued to stare with silent admiration.

Hamid took his seat next to Emma and looked at her in the mirror as the Imam left the podium and quietly said, "You may now show your face to your new husband."

Emma reached for her veil and lifted it up and back. In the mirror, Hamid saw the vision of beauty that would be forever stamped in his memory.

CHAPTER TWENTY-THREE

April 15, 1988, Tehran, Iran—Seven Years Later

Emma was still standing, staring at the dead man on the floor, when her neighbor Aiysha stormed in. Aiysha had heard the commotion, and what she saw when she opened the kitchen door was horrifying. Emma was just standing there, her burka hanging from her shoulder, her breast exposed. A dead man lay face up on the floor, a knife embedded in his chest, blood seeping and pooling near the body.

"Hamid is dead," Emma said in a steady voice, as she continued staring at the man on the floor.

"But... but... " said Aiysha, her head spinning. "This is not Hamid!" She gestured to the man on the floor.

"No, he is from the Republican Guard," said Emma, still staring at the man. "He is the one that delivered the message that Hamid was killed in the war, then he tried to rape me, using a sighe contract to legitimize his sickness... I grabbed a knife and threw it, and now he is dead, too."

Both women stared at each other as the reality of the situation sunk in, then Aiysha said firmly, "You must leave here quickly or you will be dead too. I have a cousin visiting who might help. I must report this within a reasonable time or I will be dead as well. Please hurry and gather your things and your girls. I will return in five minutes. Hurry!"

Emma knew that Aiysha's family was not completely in agreement with the revolution. Their family had lost status and assets when the Shah was deposed. They could only pretend that they all were happy with the changes, or they were sure to be taken in the night. Anyone suspected of collaborating with the Shah or the Savak secret police disappeared quickly, never to be seen again.

As Aiysha hurried back to her home, her mind was on fire, analyzing what she had just seen and trying to determine the proper thing to do. Her family had all agreed to play along with the new government and not create any problems for themselves, but the dead man lying on the floor in a pool of blood was different. Attempting to rape a woman could not be tolerated. Even at great personal risk, Aiysha was going to help.

Emma quickly gathered some things in a bag and strapped together a swaddling blanket to carry the girls in, one on each hip. She went to the cupboards and gathered as much food as she could carry, and collected some cloth diapers and basic medicines. It would have to do.

She hurried into the bedroom where the girls were still thankfully sound asleep. She grabbed her father's folding knife from her nightstand and tucked it into the shoulder bag. It was her favorite knife, easily concealed and well-balanced. She grabbed the warmest blanket she could find and quickly filled another shoulder bag with some clothes and other useful items.

She then gently lifted each sleeping girl into the hip slings and worked her way back into the living room. She stood at the window, peering outside for signs of Aiysha.

Soon a vehicle rumbled up the dark, narrow, cobblestone street. It was a flatbed truck overloaded with boxes, which looked like it should have stopped running years ago. A man got out and Emma saw Aiysha rush over to him. They looked in both directions, then hurried to her door. Emma opened it before they knocked and they entered, shutting the door silently behind them.

"Emma, this is my cousin Eyelle," Aiysha said quickly in a low voice. "He is from the Azerbaijan district, near the Turkish border. He should be able to get you there."

Eyelle walked to the kitchen and looked at the dead man on the floor. He then spit on him and said, "I shit on your father's soul!" in Persian, which Emma did not fully understand due to his accent, but the spitting and 'shit' word she did. His words convinced her that he was on her side, which would make it easier to get in the truck with him.

Emma said to Aiysha, "Can you get a telegram sent?"

"Probably, yes," said Aiysha. Emma quickly grabbed a pen and paper and wrote a message and handed it to her.

"Here, send this as quickly and secretly as possible." She looked her friend in the eye, then stepped forward for a hug. "Thank you Aiysha. I love you very much. God be with you."

Aiysha smiled and started to cry. "And you as well." They hugged. Aiysha placed her hands on the heads of the now fidgeting girls on Emma's hips and gave them each a gentle kiss.

Emma quickly loaded the two sleepy, protesting girls into the truck. Aiysha stepped back from the truck, and together with their new friend the small family rumbled down the street.

CHAPTER TWENTY-FOUR

April 16, 1988, Washington, DC
CIA Director Andrew Moyles' office

Director Moyles always preferred knocks on the door to phone calls or intercom announcements. People around him knew this. He had learned to recognize his subordinates' knocks, and could generally tell who was behind the door.

He was old-school when it came down to it, and relied on the smart young people around him to do the computer and technical work. If he had his way, these new computers would be just for fun or home use, and communication would be by phone or with a typewriter, or better yet in person. But it was a changing world, and changing fast. The world was getting complicated.

Among that morning's notes was a brief about a woman he was soon to meet. He had never heard her name before, and he had not spoken with Vice Director Jim Athan about her yet. But the brief mentioned that it had to do with Hamid Aroundami, a name the director was vaguely familiar with.

He recognized Jim's knock on the door. "Come!"

Jim, a tall, clean cut man with a dark suit and stripped tie and square glasses, stepped into the office and shut the door behind him. "Good morning, sir."

"We don't have much time," the director responded gruffly. "I need more information on the Molly Andrade meeting."

Jim sat across from him, the sunrise shining through the window creating a red glow in the room. "It involves a woman named Emma Nicholson. She married Hamid Aroundami in Washington State around seven years ago. They met when he was in med school in Seattle. He switched majors to nuclear engineering, then she ended up in med school herself. Emma is half Iranian on her mother's side, but her mother died here in the States a few years before she left for Iran. Her father was Eric Nicholson, one of the embassy hostages during the crisis back in '79. He died of cancer a couple of weeks after being released. A year or two later Ms. Nicholson and Aroundami got married, she and Aroundami had twin girls here. Shortly thereafter, they disappeared to Iran together."

The director raised his eyebrows. "What do you mean, 'disappeared'?"

"He was working at the Hanford Nuclear Reservation in south-central Washington State. Apparently he was well liked and smart as hell. He was given a lot of access, probably more than he should have been given. Now, the plant is being decommissioned and they're just in cleanup mode, but there was a lot of plutonium produced there over the years. He would have had access to information detailing how to make plutonium. When we found out an Iranian national was working there, we went and interviewed him. It seemed he was just working on decommissioning. Then a week after the interview, he and his wife and girls jumped on a plane for Iran."

The director sighed. "And do we know what he was doing in Iran?"

Jim nodded. "For a year or so there was nothing. Then this Aroundami character starts showing up on our radar. He seems to be highly regarded, but we really don't know what he is doing. During the revolution they executed most of the talented people in the Shah's regime, so they would need someone with his expertise. Bringing back a US-trained nuclear engineer was a pretty big coup for them."

"Great," said the director, shaking his head in disgust.

Jim nodded again, acknowledging the irony. "So, once they were in Iran his wife Emma completely fell off the radar. Not a word, no contacts with anyone that we know of... not even a rumor for two years, then I got a call last night, from an old friend of mine in Seattle, Molly Andrade. She was best friends with Emma's mother—apparently they went to college together. She told me a story about a telegram that she received yesterday, and requested an audience with me. Her description of it aroused my attention, so I asked her to hop on a red-eye last night from Seattle. She'll be worth a listen, I believe."

As if on cue, the director's assistant knocked, then poked her head in. "Mrs. Andrade is here."

The director said to Jim, "Let's see what she has to say. I hope this is worth our time."

Molly entered the room, a silver-haired woman, small in stature but dignified. Jim rose to greet her. "Hello, Molly.".

"Hello, Jim. It has been a while," Molly said, grinning broadly as she accepted a gentle hug from Jim.

"Molly, this is Director Moyle, head of the CIA."

"My pleasure." Director Moyle smiled and came around his desk to shake Molly's hand. "Please, take a seat."

"Well," said Molly, "I wasn't quite expecting the top of the heap right from the start. I hope this is worth your while."

Laughing, Jim said, "We were just having the same thoughts, to be honest."

They all sat down as a cup of coffee was set in front of Molly by the assistant, who then left the room.

The director leaned back in his chair. "I understand you received an interesting communication from Emma Aroundami, Mrs. Andrade?"

She took a deep breath and started in. "Well, I don't know how much is known here, but Emma Nicholson is the daughter of a former good friend of mine. When she was still very young—while her father was a hostage, in fact—she married this Hamid fellow. Actually at first it was this temporary marriage thing, but that's another story. Anyway, they were extremely religious. After her father died they had twins together, back in Seattle. Soon after Emma graduated, they jumped on a plane to Iran and that was that, I didn't hear another word from her. I think the girls are around two years old now."

"And her husband is Hamid Aroundami," said the director under his breath while looking again at the brief.

"Yes, that is correct," Molly said. "Anyway, before she left, we sat down at a coffee shop together. She explained to me how he was going to take care of her and the babies, and said that they would have a wonderful life in Iran together, what a beautiful place it was, blah blah blah. Anything negative I said was just filed under 'Auntie Molly being over-concerned' type thing." Molly's tone expressed her frustration. "But I made her promise me one thing: that if anything happened and she needed to escape Iran, she would contact me and I would try to get her out. She knew I had a friend working in the CIA." She nodded at Jim.

Then she rooted around in her purse and pulled out a piece of folded paper. "So yesterday I received this." She handed the telegram to the director. It was addressed to Molly with no sender's name other than an apparent Tehran origination. It said simply, "I will be at the rendezvous point April 19 at 1 a.m. with the girls or I will be dead."

Molly went on. "The rendezvous point is at the ski hill at Kay in the western hills of Iran, near Turkey. I don't even know if it still exists—it's a small speck of a town near the Turkish border. Her family visited there once when she was young, when the Shah was still in power, and they skied at the place. I remember her mom telling me the story. When Emma and I were having our coffee, that is the spot we agreed to. At the time, she thought I was being ridiculous."

Molly looked down at her hands a moment, then looked back up with narrowed eyes. "I believe that something desperate has happened, and that she will be there at one a.m. on April 19."

The director read the telegram. After a thoughtful pause, he said, "So what you are telling me is that the wife of Hamid Aroundami wants to defect?"

Molly angrily shot back, "Is 'defect' what you call it when she is an American citizen?"

The director met her eyes. "No. You're right. My apologies." He set the telegram on his desk. "Is there anything else that could be useful to us, any other communication, rumors, anything?"

Molly shrugged. "I haven't heard anything. But then again, I wouldn't. Communicating with people in the U.S. right now if you're in Iran isn't a real safe thing to do. I have been worried about her since she left. But there is one other thing about Emma you should know."

"Yes?" said the director.

"Well, she is good with knives," said Molly.

"Excuse me?" The director and Jim exchanged glances.

Molly continued, "Knives. She took this self-defense class after she and Hamid had a problem with a crazy neighbor. She became obsessed. The teacher was this ex-Green Beret guy who took her on as a special project. He taught her how to use knives in self-defense."

The director looked at Jim with his eyebrows raised. Jim just shrugged.

Molly continued, "Anyway, one day Emma came over for a backyard tea party and book club with some friends of mine. We were all having a lovely time, and we got on the subject of her self-defense work and convinced her to show us all something. She asked for a knife, so I brought out my block of kitchen knives. She felt the knives, pulled one out that she seemed to like, and flipped it a few times. Then before anyone knew it, with a scream she flung the knife across the yard into my lovely Douglas Fir tree. It had to be twenty feet away. The knife struck dead center, chest high. It was the freakiest thing I have ever seen."

Molly took a sip of her coffee. "Every person at the party was just standing there in stunned silence, staring at Emma. She was standing there with her lovely hijab on, with this odd, satisfied smirk on her face as she looked at the knife. She walked over, pulled the knife out of the tree, slowly wiped it off with a napkin, and replaced it in the block. She picked up her cup of tea and went on like nothing had happened. End of story."

"Huh," said the director. Is there anything else you can tell us about her?"

Molly shook her head. "Not really. Just that she's one of the most determined people I've ever known. Once Emma makes up her mind to do something, it happens. If she's ready to leave Iran she'll be at that rendezvous spot."

"Ok, well thank you for coming in," said the director, standing. "Have a safe trip home. Please speak with my assistant, we will be taking care of your traveling expenses, and I'll have Jim give you any updates we can release. This must be kept at the highest level of secrecy."

"I understand," said Molly.

Jim went out with her to say goodbye, then returned to the director's office and shut the door behind him.

"What's your impression, Jim. Do you think this is real?" The director said, both men sitting back down.

Jim said, "If it was an Iran intelligence thing and Emma is working with the regime, what are they trying to accomplish?"

They stared at each other. "I see your point," said the director.

"She had to have sent the telegram," Jim said. "Nothing else makes sense. She wants to escape, but escape from what? She didn't mention Aroundami. My guess is he's either dead or in jail."

"Is it possible their intelligence services are up to something?"

"Yes sir, it is possible. We just don't have enough working intelligence there to know anything confidently about the inner circle. We have a few Kurds in the Western province that could be of help. Most of the Kurds hate the regime, but the Turks don't like the Kurds; they consider them terrorists. In fact, it would have been challenging for her to get a secret message out. She must have had help from someone, and likely someone not friendly to the regime."

"Jim, what does your gut tell you?"

Jim thought for a moment, then looked straight at the director. "I think Emma Aroundami sent this message of her own free will, and wants out of Iran. I don't know why she wants out, but I think it's real."

The director nodded. "I agree. Next question, is she worth the risk?"

Jim looked down at his hands thinking then looked directly at the director and said, "If Aroundami is who we think he is, yes I believe she is worth the risk. We need to know what she knows. We have so little intelligence regarding their nuclear program, it seems like this is our chance to learn some things."

"OK then, let's move on this," said the director. "I want the wife and daughters of Hamid Aroundami back on American soil, whatever it takes."

"Yes sir," said Jim.

"And Jim," the director added. "One last thing. That brief this morning didn't mention anything about Emma's fondness for knives... I don't care if she is an expert with fucking chopsticks, we need to know everything about this woman. Light a fire under the background check crew and let's get this right, please," he growled. "I want you and Steve and Tom back in my office in one hour, and I want a breakdown of the best options available.. and let's find that Green Beret fellow who taught her how to throw a knife. Get him here now."

"Yes sir."

"And get a brief to the NSC prepared ASAP, I want them on board."

"I understand," said Jim, as he stood and left the room.

After Jim left, the director pushed his intercom button and said, "Alicia, get me the president on the line, priority one."

CHAPTER TWENTY-FIVE

As Eyelle and Emma drove away from the crime scene, Emma took one last look at Aiysha, then she was out of sight. Eyelle started talking quickly in Persian in a heavy, unfamiliar accent.

"We need to get out of Tehran quickly. I know some roads where we should not run into any checkpoints," he said.

"Please," said Emma. "Talk slower. My Persian is not perfect and you have a strong accent. Are you Kurdish?"

"Yes, sorry," said Eyelle more slowly. "My tribe is from the Azerbaijan region. If we make it there, you will be safe, but between here and there is the tricky part."

"Do you know where Kay is?" asked Emma.

"Yes. I have made deliveries there before. They had a ski hill there during the Shah years."

"Yes, yes!" Emma said excitedly. "That is it!"

"Why is this important?" asked Eyelle.

Emma thought for a moment, not sure how much information to release to this man she just met. Ultimately she decided that her life was in his hands and she would just have to trust him.

"It is my rendezvous point in three days. Some friends will meet me there and take us out of Iran." She looked at the sleeping girls. "That is, if my message gets out, if it falls into the right hands, and if they decide that I am worth rescuing."

"I am assuming that 'they' are the Americans, and the fact that you apparently killed that Republican Guard back there means the Guard will soon be looking for you."

Emma sighed at the reality of her situation. "Yes, that about covers it."

"If you are caught by the Guard you will be tortured and killed, they do not show a lot of mercy when it comes to someone killing one of their own, I don't care what he did." Eyelle said in a monotonous and unsympathetic voice.

"Thank you for that clarification. But that man needed to die—he was no Muslim, he was a pig," said Emma firmly.

Eyelle stared straight ahead thinking. "There are good Muslims and bad ones. I suspect this is true of all religions. It is a sad world that we live in sometimes."

His insight was good, Emma thought. She was comfortable being with him, he felt stable and bright. The girls were starting to stir and Savanna whimpered, "I'm hungry."

"We will eat soon, sweet one, just a little farther. You are being so good." Emma handed Savanna a tea biscuit that she happily started nibbling on.

Just then, they came around a bend in the road and there was a roadblock in front of them. A lone guard leaning against a tree raised his gun and pointed it directly at Eyelle. Eyelle brought the truck to a stop. The guard slowly approached the door, gun at the ready. Eyelle noticed his finger was on the trigger.

"Papers!" the young man yelled.

"Yes," said Eyelle nervously, "I have them somewhere here." He was reaching for the gun at his hip, when Emma spoke up.

"Here, I have them." She reached into her bag, pulled out a stack of bills, and handed them to Eyelle, who looked down at them, shrugged, and passed them to the guard. The guard took the money, considering the stack of bills in his hand. He peered into the truck, then looked back at the money. He then lowered his gun, walked over to the road block, and moved the barriers to let them pass.

They drove through. Once out of sight, Eyelle released a pent-up breath. "That was helpful."

"Yes," said Emma. "But that was half of what I have."

"Well," said Eyelle. "We are coming to the countryside, so your money should go further. Bribing is much more expensive the closer you are to Tehran."

They both burst out laughing. It was good for Emma to laugh, even if for a moment, to take her mind off the hell she had been through. The day was wearing her down, but she knew she had to stay strong and alert to have any chance of her daughters surviving.

As the girls were snuggled on the seat next to her, dozing fitfully, Emma leaned into the door and propped up a blanket for herself. Within a few minutes, she too was asleep.

Eyelle looked at her as he drove down the quiet road, wondering what he had stumbled into. He had some time to just think, and the more he thought, the more he realized their situation was dire. She had killed a Republican Guard. He had seen the dirty work, as had his cousin Aiysha. When the Guard found the dead man, Eyelle knew they would stop at nothing to find his killer—this woman sitting next to him. Aiysha would be in dire trouble whether she had helped in the escape or not—in fact, everyone who knew Emma would be in trouble. Therefore, he reasoned, since they would all be in trouble whether or not they were actually helping her, they might as well help.

If they could make it to Hoshi's house in Maragheh, they could hide the truck and stay with him for a couple of days, which would give them time to plan the rest of Emma's escape. The rendezvous time was still two nights away, and they would be only a four-hour drive from the rendezvous point. He gripped the wheel tighter, fighting his own fatigue. All he had to do tonight was get to Hoshi's house.

They arrived in Maragheh shortly before dawn.

"Emma, wake please," Eyelle said gently, startling her awake.

It took a moment for Emma to gain her thoughts, then she asked, "Where are we?"

"We are getting close to Maragheh. I have a cousin there who will help us. We are in Azerbaijan at this point—it is a little friendlier, but I'm sure they've found the dead man back there now and the Guard will have many people searching for you. We will stay with my cousin and his family." He smiled over at her. "They will be glad to help us; they hate the Republican Guard. They have a farm and there are a number of buildings where we can hide the truck."

"And how do they feel about someone who is half American?" asked Emma.

Eyelle shrugged. "Hopefully you killed the right person. Maybe he didn't have so many friends."

"Well, it's not all that reassuring, but I have to trust your instinct," said Emma.

The girls, too, were stirring, looking puzzled as they woke to find themselves in the jolting truck, on an unfamiliar road. "We are almost there, sweet girls, you have both been so good," Emma said while rubbing their heads gently. She asked Eyelle to stop the truck and changed the girls' diapers on the side of the road, then gave them each a tea biscuit and a drink of water.

As they drove through the sleeping town, Emma was wishing they had arrived during the day so she could appreciate its beauty. But she was also relieved that the trip had gone relatively well, other than the close call near Tehran.

A mile or so past the town they pulled into a driveway surrounded by an orchard that looked like olive or fig trees—she was not sure in the dark. They drove several hundred yards through the orchard and came upon the house and barn compound. Lights were on in the house; it was obvious that inside, the day had already begun.

"Stay here, I need to talk with them first," said Eyelle. He walked to the house and was gone for a fair amount of time. When he reappeared he came to the passenger side of the truck and motioning her to roll down the window.

"You are in the news," he said immediately. "They are saying you killed a Republican Guard in cold blood and escaped. The man you killed was very important. If anyone sees you they are to report it immediately."

"And is the man's importance a good thing or bad thing with your cousin?" said Emma.

"It is both," replied Eyelle. "But your being here is very dangerous; he does not want anyone else to know. We must go to the back barn and stay there, out of sight. He will bring us food, and there is a bathroom and water there. Is there anything else you need?"

"It will be enough, thank you," said Emma, filled with relief. They wouldn't be turned in to the authorities—Allah must be watching over them.

Eyelle walked around to the driver's seat, got in, and pulled the truck around to the back of the barn. Emma hopped out and helped him open the heavy door at the far end of the barn, and he drove into a work room of some sort, apparently used for cleaning and boxing fruit. The room had a commercial sink and a large sorting table, and was filled with neatly stacked shipping boxes. Shelves lined the walls. There were also stacks of dried fruit in sealed containers. On the far side of the room was another door. Eyelle brought in a sleeping pad and blanket from the truck, and set up a small bed on the floor for Emma and the girls.

"I'm going to see my cousin and try to get as much information as I can. I will be back. Lock the door behind me. When you hear two knocks, then one, you know it is me." He rapped his knuckles on the wall to show what he meant. "We will bring food as soon as we can."

"Thank you, Eyelle. I am thankful that Allah has brought you into my life," Emma said spontaneously.

Eyelle looked at her, nodding as he put his hand over his heart but unable to speak, obviously touched by her words.

After Eyelle left, Emma set about taking care of the girls. So far there had been very little complaining or crying. Even though the girls had just turned two, they somehow seemed to know the importance of what was happening and were following Emma's every word. She found some towels and did her best to clean everyone up. Before long, there was the correct knock at the door. Emma unbolted it and slowly drew it open a crack. Outside stood Eyelle, with two women behind him. All had their hands full with wonderful-smelling food, obviously just made.

"These are the wives of my cousin," said Eyelle. "This is Asma and this is Mitra."

"Hello, thank you for your hospitality, it is most appreciated," Emma responded in her best Persian, opening the door wide so they could enter with the plates. The two women nodded and smiled at Emma, their attention turning toward the girls as soon as they set down the food. Eyelle found a table and some chairs from the back room and set up a makeshift dining table, and they all worked together to lay out the meal. Emma was thrilled with the complexity of the meal despite the early hour, and they set about eating.

"They say you are wanted, and killed a Republican Guard," said Mitra. "Is it true?"

Emma looked at Eyelle, but he just shrugged as he was eating his bread, indicating it was fine for her to talk. Emma turned back to Mitra and said in a steady voice, "I received a letter saying that my husband was killed in the war. The man who delivered it was an evil man from the Republican Guard; he wanted to force me to sign a sighe contract and have sex with him. When I wouldn't, he tried to force himself on me, and I killed him. So yes, I'm sure they are looking for me, but perhaps they are giving reasons that are not true."

Both women stared at her in shock. "It is so hard to know the truth anymore," said Asma.

A knock on the door startled everyone. Eyelle jumped up and said, "Yes?"

"It is Hoshi, let me in." Eyelle opened the door for his cousin, and shut it behind him. The newcomer, a roughly dressed man in his fifties, had a paper in his hand. He showed it to Eyelle, who studied it briefly then handed it to Emma.

"They are posting these around town," Hoshi said. "Somehow they know you were headed in this direction."

Emma looked at the poster. It was an old picture, but it was her. It said: "Wanted. If you see this woman, immediately contact your local authority. She is traveling with two small children. She is wanted for the murder of a Republican Guard member."

Eyelle sat down and resumed eating. Hoshi and his wives looked at each other, and a silence engulfed the room. Hoshi broke the silence. "How far do you have to travel?"

Eyelle shrugged. "Probably three or four hours, if the roads are clear. We need to leave tomorrow night by nine, earlier if the roads are bad."

"Once you leave, you will likely be stopped at least once," Hoshi said. "What if she wore a niqab or burka?"

Emma hated the thought of wearing the full face-covering burka. Typically these outfits were completely concealing, with mesh for the eyes. But she was listening.

Eyelle said, "If we are stopped, they would probably have her show her face if she wore only a niqab. But perhaps not if she was in a burka. There are tribes in the area that do commonly wear the burka, so it would not be so unusual."

Asma, who had been focused on feeding and helping the girls, looked at Hoshi and said, "Please, if I may speak?" Hoshi nodded permission. "Perhaps we could use heavy makeup so she would not be recognized. That way, if the face is shown they still might not match her to the picture... and perhaps we could fake a sighe contract, as if Eyelle had picked her up in Tehran for a little fun back home."

Hoshi gave his wife a perplexed look, then started chuckling. But after another moment's thought he shrugged and asked Emma, "What do you think?"

"Yes, thank you, that is a good idea," Emma said. She had reservations, considering that a sighe had gotten her into this mess in the first place, but it was a clever idea, and she hadn't come up with anything better. "Perhaps it could be a three-month sighe at, say, ten gold coins per week?" she suggested.

"Much too much for a prostitute from Tehran," blurted Eyelle. As soon as the words came out of his mouth he realized he'd said too much. "Not that I would know the price exactly, and not that you are a prostitute," he hastened to add. He looked down, focusing on his food, while the women stared at him.

"How about this?" said Emma. "Have the agreement read ten gold coins plus housing and food in Azerbaijan and a return trip to Tehran at the end of the agreement. This, I think, would make sense. We could say that is the reason I am returning from Tehran with you."

"That might work," said Eyelle. "Especially if you look like a prosti... " He again caught himself before finishing.

"It is all right," said Emma, "I will be a prostitute for a day if it gets me and the girls out alive."

The whole room laughed. Emma added, "I think this all makes sense, but what of my girls? They cannot be seen or it will be obvious who I am." There was silence as they all sat thinking, then Emma continued. "Is there a way we could hide them in the back of the truck? I have some medicine that I could give them so they would sleep. As long as there is air they should be OK, and they could fit in a pretty small space."

Eyelle nodded. "Yes, we could do that. The truck is full of crates of canned food that I am taking back. We could set up a secret compartment for them in the middle. Without seeing the children, the authorities would be less likely to require you to show your face." He turned to Hoshi. "Is the niqab you have one piece all the way, or is the headdress separate?"

"One piece, I think. The face scarf folds around," said Hoshi. The women nodded in agreement. "All right." Hoshi looked toward his wives. "Help Emma with the niqab, and see if you can find one of the sighe contracts that we used before. Maybe we can make it look like it is for them. It doesn't have to be perfect. We need it to be from a poor neighborhood, in fact, so that if she doesn't have traveling papers it is not a concern either. Eyelle and I will work on the secret compartment. We can change the look of the truck a bit also, in case they have a description."

The men soon left and Emma sat with Asma, Mitra and the girls. The girls seemed to be greatly enjoying the attention the two young wives were paying them. Emma was curious how they had both become married to Hoshi.

Although not illegal in Iran, it was unusual for a man to have two wives, at least in Emma's experience. It required a hard worker or a well-off man, since he had to be able to provide for both wives.

Emma was thinking of a way to break the silence as they cleaned up the morning meal, and as she helped Asma put away the plates said, "Hoshi seems nice. Have you been married long?"

Asma shook her head. "Only one year. Mitra and I were best friends when Hoshi started dating her. We were living in Tehran and he wanted to bring Mitra back here as his wife, but we could not stand the idea of being apart, so we actually suggested he take both of us. Our families were happy too, as both of our families are very poor. There was not much of a dowry, but Hoshi did not care; the happiness of receiving two young brides overcame his desire for riches."

Emma chuckled and Asma smiled as well. "He has been a good provider and we are both very happy so far, but as I said, it has only been a year. Getting used to living on the farm has been challenging, but it is quite beautiful as well. The war has been good for us, actually; there is a lot of demand for dried fruits. Overall, life has been good." Her smile faltered then, and she blurted out, "I worry that you will be trouble for all of us."

Mitra made a hushing noise, glaring at Asma.

"I'm sorry," Asma said. "We want to help you, it is just that it is very frightening. It is a very serious charge against you."

"I know," Emma said. "And I cannot thank you enough. Ever since it happened, I have considered turning myself in to avoid trouble for others, but I must do everything I can so that my girls have a mother."

Asma nodded, "Yes, I understand. We will try our best to help, and by the grace of Allah we will be protected, as it is the right thing to do."

"Thank you." Emma smiled and put her hand on Asma's. She realized the great risk they were taking and she, too, hoped that they wouldn't be punished for helping.

"Our lives changed a lot after the revolution," said Asma. "Our family really wasn't that religious—we thought the revolution was good from a national standpoint, but when the Islamists took over and the Ayatollah came back, life was hard. We had to learn so many new things, and let go of so many things that we were used to. Why did they ban music? I still do not see the sense of that, nor will I ever. But things seem to be getting a little better. When we go into Tehran, it seems like there is a little more hope."

Emma was impressed with Asma's insights, especially since the girl had never been to a western country. "Well," said Emma. "The restrictions are difficult, but in the west sometimes too much freedom can be a bad thing, too. I am torn at times about leaving, but I must because of what I have done. I do love Iran very much."

They looked at each other and smiled. Asma added, "I think our two peoples are more alike than our leaders know."

The truck was parked off to the side in the barn-like structure, where Hoshi and Eyelle were changing the look of the truck as best they could. They decided to paint the truck and the bed siding. For the truck body, Hoshi brought in some brownish paint that was usually used for the olive tins, and they used some leftover house paint to spruce up the wood railings on the sides.

They unloaded the truck and took rough measurements to figure out the box for the girls. Eyelle realized that they could leave some air holes underneath, and line them up with the off-center floorboards of the truck bed to give some air flow. They nailed the box to the floor to make sure it didn't shift. They then cut a hose and ran it to the side as a backup, and stacked boxes around it. With some trial and error they were able to put together a reasonably hidden compartment that was satisfactory to both of them. Then they re-stacked the boxes to make sure they hadn't missed anything. It would have to do.

The space for the girls was small, about three feet by three feet, but it would be plenty of room for the two of them to snuggle up. If they woke up, Emma knew it would be a problem. She could only hope the sedatives she had would work for the three or four hours it would take them to get to Kay.

They set up some bedding and blankets, and started to stack the boxes of dried fruit around it, leaving the lid for the last. As the time to leave approached, Emma gave the girls the sedatives, figuring a third of a pill each would be enough. The thought of them waking up while in the box sent shivers down her spine, but she knew too much medication could cause permanent harm to a two-year-old.

The niqab was a long, flowing garment with a wrap around Emma's face. When it was closed, only her eyes were exposed. She was not used to the face covering and left it open, but practiced closing it quickly if needed.

Asma and Mitra had gone to work on Emma's face. It was helpful that she never wore makeup—the picture on the wanted poster really didn't look like her once she was covered in foundation, blush, lipstick and eye pencil. She looked in the mirror and hardly recognized herself.

"Thank you, cousin," Eyelle said to Hoshi as they prepared to leave.

"Allah will be with you, cousin," Hoshi replied. "I am sure we are doing the right thing. It is a just cause."

They hugged, each wondering if it would be for the last time.

They loaded the drugged girls into the tiny crate. Emma reached down and tucked the blankets around them, gently stroking their hair. She turned and looked at Eyelle, terrified. He watched her with sympathetic eyes until she nodded and moved away. Eyelle gently placed the lid on the crate. They extended the hose, then stacked the remaining boxes around the secret compartment.

Emma watched as the boxes were stacked higher and higher, then they were lashed down tightly with many ropes. They all worked silently, fully aware of the gravity of the situation.

Emma and Eyelle quickly said their goodbyes and got into the truck. They drove down the dark road, through the orchard and onto the pavement, heading toward Kay.

CHAPTER TWENTY-SIX

CIA Headquarters, Washington, DC

The four men in the room settled in around the conference table: Director Moyles, Jim Athan, Head of Intelligence Operations Tom Reger, and Head of Special Operations Steve Hammond.

Director Moyles opened the meeting. "Gentlemen, the president and the NSC have approved this mission. We will extract Emma Aroundami from the rendezvous point in Kay." He turned to Jim. "Where are we at?"

Jim referred to his notes. "We found the Green Beret knife trainer. His name is John Chapman."

"Christ," cut in the director. "Let me guess, the same one from the Iran hostage rescue team."

"Yep," replied Jim. "He retired after that, moved to Seattle, and started a self-defense school, where he met our Ms. Nicholson. He has been keeping himself busy, apparently has stayed in peak condition. A couple of points that are pretty important about the man, he speaks fluent Persian, and is half Hispanic, so he could pass for an Iranian. He is probably a better fit than most of the special ops guys that we have available. He says his accent leans more toward Kurdish Persian, which is where we are going. He is still in the reserves and trains once a month. He was pretty excited to hear from us, it sounds like he is anxious and ready to help. We didn't tell him who it is we are rescuing yet."

"Where is he now?" asked the director.

"He's on his way, sir," Jim said. "We have a car waiting for him at the airport. He should be here in a couple of hours."

"The Kurds are fairly widespread in The Western Azerbaijan Province," said Tom Reger. "They are not especially friendly with the Islamic regime in that province, plus they are mostly Sunni."

"Your point, please," said the director.

"Well, we know that Kay is the rendezvous point, and we know the telegram was sent from Tehran. She has a long ways to go, maybe four hundred miles. If she is getting help, it could be a Kurd, or someone at least friendly with the Kurds and not so friendly with the regime. Not only do the Kurds hate the regime and want their independence, but they are primarily Sunni Muslim, which makes for an extremely tense religious balance with Shiite leadership in Iran."

Reger paused a moment, then continued. "Iraq thought this too, and tried to recruit the Kurds to revolt and join the Iraq side of the war, but so far Iranian nationalism seems to be winning out. The Kurds are no friends of Saddam Hussein, either. Even though much of the leadership of his army is Sunni, many of the recruits are Shiite. They are fighting more for nationalism than religion, but even that doesn't add up. In other words, it is a convoluted mess in that area right now."

Head of Special Operations Steve Hammond spoke up at this point. "So if we assume she is on the run for some unknown reason, and the Republican Guard is after her, even if she makes it out of her neighborhood, she is going through a war zone carrying a couple of two-year-old girls and being chased by people that really don't want her to escape." He shook his head. "Women in Iran don't just walk around by themselves with a couple of two-year-olds in tow. I can't imagine a scenario where she could even get out of Tehran, let alone make it to the Turkish border. She'll have to jump from region to region, language to language, tribe to tribe. We are putting a lot of faith in her ability to navigate some pretty rough waters."

Tom nodded. "True, but if she is able to get away from Tehran, and is able to get up into the Azerbaijan region, she would be around a lot more sympathetic people."

"Well, it does seem logical that she has some help," interjected Jim. "And also logical that they would be Kurds. We do have a few connections with the Kurds in Azerbaijan."

Hammond said, "The Turkish border is not heavily guarded. Most of their resources are dedicated to the Iraq border. If she is able to get there, we could get a small rescue team to Kay without being detected, I believe."

Just then came a knock at the door. The director's assistant cracked the door, peeked her head in and said, "It's a Mr. Ono from communications, sir. You said to alert you if it sounded important."

"Show him in," said the director.

A young sliver of a man walked in, obviously nervous. "I'm sorry to interrupt, sir," he said to Reger, who nodded his head indicating it was OK.

"That's all right. Introduce yourself," said the director, observing the interaction between the two.

The newcomer turned to Director Moyles. "Steven Ono, communications trainee. My mother is Iranian, I speak fluent Persian. I've been listening to communications out of Iran. I was told by Mr. Reger if I picked up any chatter that sounded odd, I needed to bring it to his attention immediately."

"Ok, what sounded odd?" the director said, getting to the point.

"Well, the Republican Guard in Tehran seem to be looking for a woman and her children. Apparently, a high-ranking officer of the Republican Guard was killed by a knife, Farzad Rostami. It's unusual because in two months on this assignment, I've never even heard a mention of a woman in Iran. They seem to be in quite a panic over this, it seems as though she is the one that killed the dude."

Everyone in the room grew stone-faced, quietly looking at each other.

"Thank you, Mr. Ono," said the director. "Good work. Report directly to Mr. Reger. Now, get back to doing what you do. We will need you to stay with it twenty-four seven for the next few days, so make arrangements."

After Ono left, the men were silent. The director spoke. "What do we have on Rostami, who is he?"

Reger said with an excited voice, "That guy is at least number two in the hierarchy of the guard, he was instrumental in setting up Hezbollah in Lebanon, the Israelis have wanted him dead for some time now."

The director continued, "OK, so if the woman referred to is Emma Aroundami, we can now assume that she is on the run because she has killed Farzad Rostami with a knife. We are also assuming that she could have some help, although we don't know that yet. Let's proceed as if she will make it to Kay with the two children in tow, and plan accordingly. If we pick up chatter that she has been captured or killed, we pull the plug on the whole operation. But until we know otherwise, we'll proceed. At least as of now she is alive and on the run—that in and of itself is impressive. Steve, what do we have for resources in that area?"

"Well," said Hammond. "We have a small special operations base about twenty clicks from the Turkish border, around sixty miles from Kay. It really is just a landing pad and a gas tank. It's pretty isolated. Only a few people in the Turkish government even know about it. They like to keep these things pretty quiet."

"Back to the Kurdish problem," said Reger. "If the Turks find out the Kurds are helping us, it's game over. They won't help us, nor will they let us proceed. We have one new special operations Little Bird helicopter at our main air base in Turkey that can handle night operations. The Little Bird can hold up to six people, plus the pilot. Lightly armored, but very tough birds, the best night technology we've got. We have special ops people at our air base in Turkey, but none there currently with night training. We can bring in some Night Stalkers from the 160th in Kentucky. Another thing: Turkey and Iran are getting to be big trading partners again, and no one wants to screw that up. So the Turks won't approve us going across with special ops, period. Also, it will be pitch black that night, no moon, and the weather can be sketchy. It's below zero now at night, but that Little Bird can fly in almost any weather, night or day, unless it's a blizzard... it is as good as we've got."

"OK," said the director. "What about Kurdish help? Can we quietly make some inquiries to find out if we can get someone in there to help ahead of time? And is there any way of finding out if she is already getting some help without raising any Iranian suspicion that we're on to it?"

Tom Reger spoke up. "It is hard to know who we can trust—we are not always right on that one. But if the Kurds recognize a situation that would piss off someone high in the Republican Guard, they would have recruits lined up for the job. Again, confused lines. Turkey doesn't want the Kurds, the Islamic regime doesn't think they are Islamic enough, and the Kurds are smart enough to know that Saddam Hussein is no solution, but then they are still loyal to the nation of Iran to a certain degree... Allegiances can change on a whim in that area. It's all about tribal deal making."

Athan said, "So what if we send in Chapman, and say a team of two Night Stalkers with him, and two choppers: a Little Bird and a Blackhawk. We go across the border with the Little Bird with Chapman, two Night Stalkers and the pilot, and have the Blackhawk as a firepower backup that stays on the Turkish side. We could go across with both birds, but that would give us a better chance of getting spotted."

The director jumped in sharply. "We go across with one helicopter, the second on standby only. This is going to be tight and small, nothing that can implicate us. The team will be on their own, and that order comes directly from the top. The president does not want a media show in the Iranian press if something goes wrong. We could have plausible deniability of a rogue mission."

"What about the Turks?" asked Reger.

"We could tell the Turks that we are going to our forward base to restock the fuel there and practice our night training," said Jim.

The director looked around the room and all seemed to be in agreement. "OK, then, we have a working plan."

At midnight there was another knock on the door of the director's office. The four had gathered again, the plan now firmly in place.

"Yes," said the director. An obviously exhausted assistant poked her head in and told him John Chapman had arrived.

"Right, send him in. And Ms. Kingman, you are free to go for the evening. Please go home and get some rest. I appreciate you staying so late."

"Thank you, sir," she said with visible relief.

John Chapman entered the room, an imposing and simply dressed man with broad shoulders and a chiseled face. His square jaw and weathered face told of a man focused and proud of himself.

He saluted. "John Chapman reporting for service, sir."

"At ease, Sergeant Chapman. Please have a seat," said the director.

"Yes sir."

"We need you to lead a team into Iran for a quick search and rescue of an American citizen," said the director. "Jim, can you take over?"

Athan said, "We obtained this telegram from Iran—it seems to be from a reliable source." He handed the telegram to Chapman. "Our confidence is high it is from a woman named Emma Nicholson, or Emma Aroundami, who moved to Iran a couple of years ago with her Iranian husband and two babies."

"Wow," said Chapman, as the realization hit him. "Let me guess—she's the same Emma Aroundami I trained in Seattle a few years back."

"Correct," said Jim. "Her husband is Hamid Aroundami, who got a nuclear engineering degree at U of Washington before they went back to Iran. We believe he is involved in Iran's nuclear bomb ambitions."

"Great," said Chapman. "We train the guy that helps blow us up."

"Yes, we have had those same thoughts," Jim said. "A day or two ago there was a killing of a high-ranking officer in the Republican Guard, and our Mrs. Aroundami is the prime suspect. There was a knife involved, and we now know that she is on the run. We do not know the status of her husband or whether he was involved."

Chapman sat there, absorbing the news, then said, "That crazy woman could throw a knife better than I could."

"We want her back on American soil," Jim said, looking directly at Chapman. "We need what she knows."

"How do we know she is still alive?" asked Chapman.

"A few hours ago we received a report about the Republican Guard mounting a search for a woman and two children. Our confidence is high that it is our Ms. Nicholson," said Athan. "We have the rendezvous point identified near the Turkish border. We believe she is trying to get there. We have a forward base in Turkey that is relatively close to the rendezvous point. Perhaps you are familiar with it—it is called Camp Blue Mountain."

"I know about it," said Chapman. "I was there a couple of times on training runs."

"Good," said Jim. "The idea is we go in, get the woman and her daughters, and get them out as quickly as possible."

Chapman chuckled and said, "Yeah, that is always the idea. My experience is that it's always trickier than planned. That area is a tribal-controlled 'no go' zone. The advantage is that the central government does not have that much control, and we are not quite as despised there as we are elsewhere."

"Well, that's a start," deadpanned the director. Everyone chuckled.

"How big will the operation be?" asked Chap.

Jim said, "We are currently putting together a team for you from the 160th Special Ops. You will have two Night Stalkers and the pilot in a Little Bird, as well as a Blackhawk that stays at Blue Mountain."

Chapman raised his eyebrows. "I've heard about the 160th. It was set up after our desert hostage fiasco, correct?"

"That's right. We've notified the commander from the Night Stalker base at Campbell Airfield in Kentucky. The team is on the way. You will be the lead, due to your direct experience in that region and also due to the fact that you know Ms. Nicholson and speak the language. You will travel later tonight non-stop, refueling midair. The idea is that we go with two helicopters—on a night training run, as far as the Turks are concerned—and get to Blue Mountain for refueling. The Little Bird goes across, gets Ms. Nicholson, and we all get back to the main base one big happy family. You have authorization to go across with only one Bird. The Blackhawk is just for emergencies, and I can't even tell you what will and won't be approved—you'll have to make your own call. You'll be briefed with everything we have on the flight. From

Blue Mountain it is around a thirty-minute flight to the rendezvous point. You go in, drop the Night Stalkers with enough time to locate her, then go back and pick everyone up. You'll have to come up with the exact plan in flight. If she's not there at oh one hundred hours, you leave."

Chapman surveyed the room, nodding. "OK, what are we waiting for?"

The men in the room all spontaneously stood and saluted. The director stood up, saluted as well, then shook Chapman's hand, "Good luck, Sergeant Chapman. The Night Stalker team should be here in a couple of hours. We are getting the plane loaded with anything your team might need."

"Thank you sir," said Chapman. He saluted again and left the room.

"Steve, you're in charge of the details. Get me updates every few hours as you can. The president will be very interested in being kept in the loop on this one. Let's all grab a bit of sleep and be back in my office at oh five hundred. Let's get this right, gentlemen."

CHAPTER TWENTY-SEVEN

Emma's simple niqab looked right. The face shield was tucked in so that only her heavily made-up eyes showed.

Eyelle had all of his papers ready, detailing his truckload of goods. They had discussed what to do if stopped, and planned how they would handle different situations. They still had Emma's remaining cash for a bribe, but using it at this point would be unlikely to work; they were now sure that Emma and the girls were wanted fugitives.

Eyelle had given no thought to his own escape after dropping off Emma. His sole focus was on delivering her to the rendezvous point. He had become solely and unselfishly dedicated to this woman that he hardly knew, although she was technically his wife, according to the sighe contract they were carrying. He chuckled out loud at that thought.

"What's funny?" asked Emma.

"Ah, just the irony of you technically being my wife, when the last man that wanted you for a sighe, is, well, you know... " his voice trailed off as he realized it wasn't that funny.

Emma chuckled anyway. "Yes, it is ironic. But I won't kill you, I have no knife." This wasn't quite the truth, because she still had her father's folding knife for emergencies. Eyelle gave her a strange look, then burst out laughing.

This was a good woman next to him. He appreciated her dark humor and fearlessness; he had never before been around a woman like her. Most women in his life were followers, mild souls, including his beloved wife who had died years ago in childbirth. He missed her more with every year, but he knew that she would be proud of what he was doing.

His life had become so absurdly monotonous that he hardly knew himself anymore. He had contemplated suicide many times, but kept going, as he did not feel that his wife or Allah would approve. Now he was on a mission. He had found the reason he was alive, and that was to deliver Emma and her children to the rendezvous point. This was Allah's mission for him, and he must not fail. As they drove, he thought about the disrespect that he had been subjected to so many times under the regime. Being Kurdish was enough to earn him treatment as a second-class citizen.

He had been a devout Muslim his whole life. But after his wife died, things changed. His daily prayers became his grieving sessions, not thinking of Allah but thinking of her. Why did Allah take her away from him?

Up until her death he had prayed and prayed and truly studied Islam. He was proud to be the perfect man, the perfect Muslim, the perfect believer. He memorized the Koran, immersing himself in the teachings of many great leaders. He did everything that he was called upon by Allah to do, but it did not help. She still died, as did his beautiful baby boy.

How, at this point, was he to bow down to a God that had so deserted him, that had left him hopeless and devoid of love? It had made him a bitter and lonely man, but still he was going through the motions, since he did not know what else to do. Emma had brought back a fire in him, a focus and desire to accomplish something, a desire that he had not felt since he first knew that he was going to be a father. His grief and anger had been displaced by a sole purpose; to fulfill this mission, to deliver from evil the woman that had been wronged, and to give her beautiful girls a chance in life.

Emma sat quietly as they moved on through the darkness. She was ready for whatever was ahead. She thought of Aiysha back in Tehran. Asma and Mitra. Would they be safe, or had she put them into great danger? It was hard to know the right thing to do, but it kept coming back to her daughters. She must survive for them. She could only hope and pray that the box they had set up and the medicine she had given them would work. If not, all of this would be for nothing. She would have no reason to live, if anything happened to her girls.

"Emma!" Eyelle said, breaking her out of her thoughts. Ahead, bright lights faced them in the road. They pulled to a stop and watched two fully armed guards walk toward them.

Eyelle lowered his window. "It is late to be driving, why are you here?" one of them demanded.

"I am returning from Tehran, I am expected tonight with my supplies," said Eyelle. The other guard poked around on Emma's side of the truck.

"And who is this woman? Why is she traveling with you?" the guard asked.

"She is my wife, we agreed to a sighe in Tehran," he said, handing him the sighe contract.

The man looked at it, then looked at Emma. "Where are the children?" the guard asked.

Eyelle shook his head. "We have no children, we just met." He did his best to sound confused by the question.

The guard looked at him with disgust. "So she is your prostitute?"

"No," said Eyelle. "She is my wife in the eyes of Islam. We have agreed, I will pay her ten gold coins. It is all proper."

The guard peered past Eyelle at Emma. "Ten gold coins? It seems you paid too much. She looks like she has been paid before." The other guard laughed loudly.

The two guards walked around the truck, poking and prodding at the boxes. They walked back to their truck together, leaving Eyelle and Emma to sit in the truck. "Did they believe you?" Emma quietly asked, a note of panic in her voice.

"It is hard to tell; I'm not sure why they are talking. Do you have the money?"

Emma reached in her bag and pulled out the remaining cash. "Why would we need to bribe them if they believe us? I worry that they may find it suspicious."

Eyelle nervously tapped the steering wheel as he looked toward the men. The two men came back to the front of the truck, guns in the ready position. The first guard went back to Eyelle's side of the truck.

"There is a woman who has murdered a Republican Guard in Tehran, do you know anything of this?"

Eyelle looked at the man. "I do not. I have been busy getting my truck loaded, as I was late. How was he murdered?"

The guard didn't answer him, just stared at Eyelle. After a few moments, he yelled "Go!" and pointed down the road.

CHAPTER TWENTY-EIGHT

The two helicopters headed out from the base for Blue Mountain, where they were given a reluctant and suspicious go ahead from the Turkish command.

"I don't think they believed our story," Chap said to the two Night Stalkers on board.

The Night Stalkers had the best night vision equipment on earth. It, and the electronics on the helicopter, were cutting edge—technology Chap had not seen in action, only heard about. There was one special heat tracing system that was supposed to be able to see a body from a half mile away in pitch black.

They arrived at Blue Mountain without a hitch, the night stalkers putting on their camouflage gear and makeup on the way. After refueling the tanks, all gathered in the small shed next to the helipad. Chap said, "We leave at twenty hundred hours. It is just under thirty minutes to the drop zone. We drop the two of you off two clicks from the rendezvous spot and you'll have just over two hours to get in position, somewhere around the base of the ski hill. The Blackhawk stays here. Radio silence. Rendezvous time is oh one hundred hours. We need to get there, get the woman and her children, and get out."

"Will it be just her, or will there be other friendlies?" asked one of the Night Stalkers.

"We can't be sure, but I'm guessing she will have someone helping her if she makes it to this point. There is no word that the Iranians have found her, so we are assuming she will be there. If she is with someone, they would probably each be carrying one of the kids, so if you get into a firefight make real sure who you're shooting at."

At ten p.m., Chap gave the order. "Let's move. When we come back for you at oh one hundred, we'll make one wide circle pass to get a visual and try to pick up some heat signals. The base of the ski lift is our target; that's our best guess as to where she will be. Use a flare for the landing zone, but wait until you hear the Bird. Light the flare whether she is with you or not. We leave as soon as everyone is on board. We give her five minutes unless we come under fire, then we make a call on the spot. Radio silence until five minutes before oh one hundred. Understood?"

"Yes sir," all on board said in unison.

After a last-minute check of their weapons they all loaded aboard. The tiny Little Bird flew in low and quiet to the drop zone and the two Night Stalkers expertly rappelled down to the forest floor without a hitch.

When they came back for the pickup they were bound to be noticed. They had to be ready and move fast. Chap was contemplating all of the contingencies, but there was just not enough intelligence to be sure of anything. It didn't seem like the ski hill would have ground-to-air firing power; most of that would be assigned to the Iraq border. It was much more likely that they would be dealing with local police, unless the Republican Guard was on Emma's trail.

The two men trudging through the knee-high snow had worked together for over seven years. They had both been involved in the liberation of Grenada in 1983, but this was their first CIA mission. Neither had been involved in the hostage rescue mission eight years prior; their unit was established after that fiasco to provide the army with special nighttime operations like the one they were on.

They had one heavily forested hill to cross to reach the drop zone, and the snow was surprisingly deep. Normally two miles in two hours would be plenty of time, but with each step the crust gave way to the weight of their packs and they would often sink thigh-deep into the snow. They located a game trail solid enough to walk on, but it took them on a longer path around the hill.

At midnight they reached a position where they could view the valley below. There was no movement as they scanned with their night binoculars, seeing the outline of what appeared to be an abandoned ski lift, a few small shacks, and various buildings farther in the distance. Down the hill, they could make out some lights of the town. The entire area was covered in snow, making it almost impossible to see the road. There appeared to be an area at the base of the ski lift that would be suitable to land the Little Bird.

They moved closer in the pitch-black night, with their night vision goggles activated and their silenced guns at the ready.

The two men glanced at each other, each knowing the other's thoughts: the lack of activity meant they had arrived unnoticed, but it also meant there was no one there to rescue.

They worked their way slowly across an open field in the darkness, heading toward what would be the landing pad. They set up in position and waited, scanning for any signs of life.

They were fifteen minutes early. After a few minutes a vehicle approached and pulled into what must have been a parking lot two hundred yards from their position. It looked like a truck loaded with boxes. As they watched, another car pulled up behind the truck, and a small, old-fashioned police light started flashing above the car.

CHAPTER TWENTY-NINE

Emma and Eyelle reached the road to Kay after midnight. They had not passed another car for some time and had been slowly gaining altitude. Snowbanks rose on either side, but the road was still relatively clear. After another mile or so the pavement ended and they were driving on a slushy mix of snow and mud.

When they reached the tiny town, the slushy mud turned to a paved, cobbled slab. They drove through the town on the narrow, two-way street. Kay had the look of a once-thriving community, with worn storefront signs advertising food and products for non-existent tourists from the now-defunct ski hill. A few lights shone from shuttered windows, and they passed the occasional parked car.

"The ski hill is at the far end of town, up the hill," Eyelle said, pointing to the darkness ahead. "It is twelve forty-five. Do you think they will be here soon?"

"If they come, yes, it will be soon," Emma replied. "If they do not, I do not know what to do. My note was without detail. It seems like the base of the ski hill would be the most likely location for us to wait."

Eyelle shuddered. They were many miles from his tribe and people. This area was Kurdish, but that would not matter if the Republican Guard was on their trail. He knew there was an army garrison nearby, but decided Emma didn't need to know. They slowly drove up the bumpy, tree lined road leading to the ski hill, coming to a level opening and they slowed to a stop. They had arrived. His mind was flipping back and forth over options when car lights appeared behind them. In his side mirror, Eyelle saw a red, rotating police light. Two figures exited the car and starting moving toward the truck.

Muffled screams sounded and both policeman stopped and listened, pulling their guns out of their holsters. Eyelle groaned silently. The children had woken up.

"Out, out, OUT!" one of the policemen yelled at Eyelle in Persian. "Both of you!"

The other policeman ran to Emma's side of the truck, gun drawn. "Out!" Emma and Eyelle stepped out and were marched out in front of the truck, into the headlights. "On your knees!" screamed one of the officers. The other man walked over to the truck and wiped his finger on its still-curing paint job. He showed it to the other officer as the muffled screams became louder.

The officer with his gun trained on Eyelle smiled at the paint on the other man's finger, glanced back at the truck and the screams, then looked at Emma.

"So, you are the American woman." He smiled a sinister smile as he instructed his partner to return to the police car to radio in to the nearby border garrison that they had found the fugitive. He stared silently at Emma and Eyelle as emergency sirens could now be heard close by and the town below seemed to be coming alive.

He then leaned over and ripped off Emma's headdress. Eyelle blurted, "We don't know what you are talking about."

The officer swung his gun back toward Eyelle, pointed it at Eyelle's forehead, and pulled the trigger. Eyelle's head jolted backward with the shot and his body collapsed.

Immediately after the shot, the policeman's head exploded. He collapsed only a few feet away from Emma. Emma dropped flat on the ground, then scuttled closer to the front of the truck, out of sight of the other policeman.

The sirens blaring from the town below were now mixing with the girls' frenzied screams. Emma willed her mind. Think!! She looked back at the two dead men. There must be a sniper close by, and whoever it was, he was trying to help her.

She reached into her pouch for the knife and quickly unfolded it, blocking out the desperate screams of her daughters. The other officer had to die.

She rose and started moving toward the back of the truck. As she did, the other policeman appeared. She threw her knife as hard as she could, but misjudged the distance. The knife hit at an angle and bounced off the man's heavy winter coat.

Had the man had military training, perhaps he would have recognized what was happening a split-second sooner. But he was just a local policeman. The possibility of a sniper in the darkness with a night vision scope simply did not cross his mind. He thought the shot that killed his partner must have come from Eyelle or Emma. As the knife bounced off his chest, he raised his gun. He did not have the hammer of the old-style revolver cocked, and the extra split-second it took to pull the trigger was enough of a delay for the Night Stalker to get in position and pull his trigger a fraction of a fraction sooner. The policeman's gun went off but the force of the bullet through his head caused his aim to pull to the left, just enough to miss Emma's heart. The bullet hit her in the right shoulder and sent her sprawling backward.

Emma jumped up, ignoring the pain spreading through her shoulder. She ran to the policeman's body, still twitching but obviously dead, and grabbed the errant knife. She stood and began awkwardly and frantically sawing at the ropes that tied down the boxes entombing her daughters, her right arm now hanging uselessly at her side.

Voices and vehicles and sirens could be heard from the town below. She turned and screamed to the darkness, "Help me!" and continued to slash at the ropes.

The Night Stalkers sprinted out of the darkness toward her. As she saw them approach she screamed, "My daughters are in a box in the middle!"

"Cover the road!" One of the night stalkers yelled as he shouldered his rifle and pulled out a knife, quickly cutting the ropes as the other soldier kneeled with his night-scoped rifle pointing down the road.

The soldier and Emma were now tearing at the boxes. Emma was completely unable to use her right arm, but continued dragging boxes off with all her might. Just as they reached the center of the truck bed, the sound of an approaching helicopter rose. The soldier ripped the boards off the box holding the terrified girls, grabbed his flare, and threw it to a level spot away from the truck. He then pulled the screaming girls out one by one.

Just then the other soldier yelled, "Incoming vehicles!"

The soldier handed one of the girls to Emma and jumped off the truck with the other girl in his arms. "Get down, flat!" he yelled as the helicopter swooped in, hovering for position.

Confused shouts came from the road below them. In the dim light Emma could make out the figures of men charging toward them in the lights of vehicles bouncing up the road. Machine-gun fire was pinging all around them as the Night Stalker fired back with deadly accuracy, slowing the advance. One of the advancing trucks crashed into a tree as chaos ensued.

The helicopter pilot started firing at the approaching trucks with his forward guns. The Little Bird landed, the wind from its rotors stirring up the loose snow and whipping Emma's hair around her face. Chap charged into the chaos from the helicopter, diving on top of Emma and her girl.

The soldier turned and screamed, "Now! Move, move!!" They quickly rose, Chap half-dragging and half-carrying Emma and her girl toward the helicopter, the soldier following with the other screaming girl tucked in his arm. The second soldier continued to methodically gun down the troops working their way up, but it was a losing battle. They reached the helicopter and piled in, the trailing soldier scrambling toward them when a barrage of gunfire sounded and he collapsed thirty feet from the door. Over the noise of the rotors, Emma could hardly hear him cry, "I'm hit!"

Amid whizzing bullets, Chap jumped out and ran to the soldier on the ground. He quickly dragged the man to the Little Bird as the helicopter opened up its forward guns.

"Go! Go! Go!" Chap yelled as he lifted the limp soldier into the fuselage and jumped in after him. The helicopter angled away, bullets still flying from below, as the Little Bird and its occupants swept into the darkness.

CHAPTER THIRTY

July 3, 1996, Seattle, WA—Eight Years Later

Emma's vacation plans were set. Ten days in the German countryside, staying at a lovely chalet near the Rhine river. She would catch up on reading, take gentle walks, and just spend the time reflecting.

After eight years of hiding from Republican Guard assassins, she figured it was time for a break. Up until now, she and the girls had avoided any close calls. The Secret Service was authorized to indirectly help protect her from assassination after she was rescued. But the CIA was frustrated by her inability to provide information about Iran's nuclear program. Hamid had never been involved in the nuclear program; so she had no information to give.

She hated having to use Emma Taylor as her name, and categorically refused to give up her hijab. Otherwise, she followed the Secret Service rules, and listened closely to her protectors. If she wanted the girls to have a mother, she knew she needed to pay attention.

She went to work for a global health network. Her job with them allowed for frequent transfers, and the company moved her and the girls to a different part of the world every six months. It was an exhausting routine and at times a heartbreaking one, but it had kept her and the girls safe. She knew that the Iranians would never stop looking for her; Rostami was too important of a figure for the Republican Guard to ever let it rest.

The girls would stay with Molly and Jim while she was gone. When she returned, they would be heading to a new posting somewhere in the world.

She arrived at the Seattle airport with her carry-on luggage. She would be traveling light and moving quickly. She walked through the doors leading to the check-in area, and stood next to a garbage can. She reached into her purse and pulled out her itinerary and tickets to Germany, and dropped them into the can. She unzipped a side pocket of her purse, pulled out a ticket to Paris, and worked her way to the check-in line.

CHAPTER THIRTY-ONE

The Hezbollah operative had received his orders; the courier had approached him with the correct code. There was never written or phone communication for operations, nothing that could be traced back to Tehran. The target was a meeting in Paris of Kurdish opposition leaders, men the Republican Guard wanted dead. Kurdish independence was a non-starter for the regime; unity and expansion of Iran's interests were the only options. The regime would never give up territory to the Kurds, nor grant them autonomy. The Kurdish opposition must be brutally and decisively stopped.

There was a potential bonus to taking out the Kurds. A regime operative in the US had planted an anonymous note with the CIA that appeared to come from a Kurdish source, requesting that the murderer Emma Aroundami attend the meeting.

CHAPTER THIRTY-TWO

Emma checked in to the small hotel a few blocks from Le Gourmand, the restaurant where the meeting of Kurdish opposition leaders was to be held.

After Emma killed Farzad Rostami, she had become somewhat of a cult hero amongst the Kurds. Rostami had been the architect of the brutal repression of the Kurds in northern Iran in the early eighties when they were pushing for autonomy. Thousands of Kurds were executed or tortured. Emma had become an unwitting and unintentional legend.

The authenticity of the invitation to the meeting could not be confirmed, and the CIA was no help other than passing along the invitation. However, she felt an obligation to go, she owed it to Eyelle and to the other Kurdish people who had helped her escape eight years prior.

In her hotel bathroom, Emma gazed into the tiny mirror above the ornate bowl used as a sink, which looked out of place in an otherwise ordinary bathroom. She removed her hijab, then thumbed through a French glamour magazine that she had picked up at the airport. She needed to look as French as possible. On the way to the hotel, she had stopped in at a second-hand shop and found an outfit that seemed to work. It was a low-cut, tight-fitting dress with a hemline that went mid-thigh. Her stockings and high heels matched nicely. She added a faux black pearl necklace and some large hoop earrings, then put her hair up, using a blow dryer for the first time in her life. As she did her makeup, she did her best to cover the deep dark eyes that betrayed her Persian roots. She looked in the mirror, and could not help remembering the trip with Eyelle, dressed as a prostitute. She was here because of the loyalty she felt to him. She owed it to Eyelle.

As she prepared to leave the room she took a final look in the full length mirror in the bedroom. She barely recognized herself. She was committing a grave sin going out like this, but any Muslim man looking at her would never believe she was Islamic. To all appearances, she was a stunningly beautiful and sexy French woman.

She left the hotel and headed for the late-afternoon meeting. She appreciated the warmth of the day, as she was simply not used to being outside with so much skin exposed. She tried to ignore the lustful looks she was receiving as she walked toward the restaurant. It was so much more comfortable with her hijab on, as men would almost turn up their noses when she passed. Bringing attention to herself was not her goal; fooling a potential Iranian assassin was. She reminded herself of that and kept walking.

She stopped half a block from the restaurant, pretending to look in a store window. Two Middle Eastern men walked by, completely ignoring her. Pedestrians criss-crossed the street. A block away, she noticed a dark man with a backpack leaning against a post. Nothing seemed out of place.

"Be wary of the ordinary," was a constant refrain from her protectors. "Your assassin will be a person that is the least suspicious. Do not trust anyone, and always have an escape route planned."

Emma casually glanced around at her surroundings. She could see the front of the restaurant, tucked into a cul-de-sac and surrounded by several other businesses. Directly across from her was a narrow alley that seemed to continue beyond to another street. Several old fire escape ladders ran up the sides of the buildings, leading to what appeared to be apartments above the businesses. A small truck drove past her and turned into the alley, then turned again and disappeared behind the buildings. The alley would be her escape route.

She tugged at her dress to cover more of her thighs, exposing more of her breasts, then lifted it back to the previous position, sighing as she took one more look in the store window's reflection. How women dressed like this was beyond her.

It was 4:20. According to the message, the meeting would have begun at four. She walked into the restaurant and scanned the room.

The restaurant was rectangular with eight or ten tables. A hallway led back to what appeared to be another room. There was another door to the left, with a sign indicating washrooms. The Kurds must be in the back room.

Three well-dressed men sat at a table to the left, speaking French. Their conversation halted as they all smiled and stared at the sexy woman who had just walked in. She looked at them flirtatiously and said "Bonjour," in perfect French, then greeted the approaching maître d' with her sexiest smile.

"Madame, you look most beautiful today. Is it just you, or will others be joining you?" he asked in French.

"Thank you. Yes, I am expecting others. Perhaps the table there?" She pointed to a table with the best view of the room.

He led her to the four-person table and suggested a seat facing away from the front door. Emma ignored him and sat on the other side of the table with her back to the wall, where she had a full view of the room in front of her. "A glass of red wine, please," she said in

French as he handed her the menu. He acknowledged the request and headed back to the kitchen.

She laid the menu on the table and walked to the bathroom. The three men stopped talking, and she could feel them looking at her again as she passed.

The bathroom door was at the end of the hallway, which had no exit door. She scanned the bathroom, which was simple and clean with one stall and a sink mounted atop an antique cabinet. The small window had a latch that opened inward, perhaps just big enough to squeeze through. She made her way back to the dining room.

Her wine was waiting for her when she returned to her seat. She sat looking at the menu as a Middle Eastern man entered and quickly made his way to the back room.

She took a sip of her wine. She had already broken so many rules, what difference did it make now? Allah would just have to understand the importance of her façade. She took a second sip, then studied the glass. She lifted it and swirled the glass, like she had seen others do. Why did they do that? She took a third sip, and noticed it had a subtle hint of cherries. She smelled the wine and noticed the cherry smell as well.

She was snapped out of her impromptu wine tasting as the waiter approached. "What may I get you, Madame?" he asked in French. She had forgotten to look at the menu, being distracted by the wine.

"Just a light dessert. What do you recommend?"

"We have a lovely chocolate brioche, it is the chef's favorite."

"Thank you, that will be fine. I'm going to see if my friends are in the back. There is another room, yes?"

"Yes Madame, there is a meeting there now. Are your friends part of that group?"

"I believe so. They are Kurdish, yes?"

"Ah, Madame, I believe so, yes. I believe they said they were from Northern Iran."

"Thank you, I will check." She smiled at the man as he turned and went to place her order.

She took one more sip, staring at the now half-empty glass. She blew out a silent breath, stood, brushed the wrinkles out of her dress, and made her way to the back room.

Interesting artwork adorned the hallway's walls, the paintings looking as if they had been there for generations. She reached the end of the hall and turned right, through an arched doorway. This room was half the size of the front room. Two tables had apparently been shifted together, with four men seated on each side. Another man sat at the end of the tables on the far side, facing Emma. The tables had been cleared of flowers and ornaments, holding only water glasses and a couple of appetizers.

The men all stopped their conversations and looked at Emma.

She took a breath and said, "You will have to excuse my appearance, it was necessary for my security. I am Emma Aroundami, of Iran, you have requested my attendance."

The men just continued to silently stare a moment, then looked at each other. The man at the head of the table stood and said "I am sorry, but we made no such request. I do not know what you are talking about. But your name is familiar. Are you the one who killed Rostami?" He asked, his voice tinged with incredulity.

Emma felt her heart racing. Something was wrong.

"Run!" It was Hamid's voice in her head.

She stumbled backward into the hallway as loud voices and a crash echoed from the front room. A man stormed down the hallway with an Uzi in his hand, throwing Emma to the floor as he burst past her and into the meeting room. Automatic gunfire started blazing as Emma scrambled on her knees down the hallway. The second gunman was screaming instructions to the kitchen crew. She could see another man at the front door as she frantically crawled to the front room. Once there, she got to her feet and raced toward the bathroom, hearing groans and screams coming from the back room.

"Where is she!" Emma heard.

"Who, who?" replied a terrified voice.

"Emma Aroundami, tell me!" Then came words Emma could not hear, followed by three shots.

She crashed into the bathroom, kicked off her heels and climbed onto the sink. She opened the window and forced her body into it, pushing off from the sink cabinet with her feet. As she did, the cabinet gave way from the wall and collapsed in front of the door, jamming it closed just as the gunman reached it.

With one great lunge, Emma forced herself out, and landed in the alley below. She could hear the man forcing his way into the bathroom as she got to her feet and sprinted down the dim alley. Bullets whizzed around her as the gunman fired blindly from the bathroom window. She turned, running up the alley as she had planned, never looking back.

CHAPTER THIRTY-THREE

September 22, 2004, Ballard, WA—Eight Years Later

Shane Merrill arrived for his six a.m. yoga class. His plans were set: yoga first, then a train ride to Bellingham to buy the motorcycle. He'd bring his gear and ride home, arriving back by early afternoon.

He was ready to take the leap from his little 250cc bike to a 1000cc beast of a bike, and had found the exact one he wanted online.

Yoga had become his religion. The strength and balance would be crucial to handling a bike that size.

Shane prided himself on staying in shape. He couldn't do much about the lack of hair on his head, or the abundance of hair growing in places most unattractive, but he took his health seriously and prided himself on being the best he could be. Three years after his divorce, the first dates seemed to come regularly; making it to a second or third date was more challenging. Either he wasn't interested, or the date wasn't interested in a forty-three-year-old divorced man living in a basement.

As he traveled north to Bellingham, he pondered living alone. He had some assets, and his house value seemed to be going up daily, but he had always envisioned himself with a partner. He'd hoped she would fall into his lap, motivate him, inspire him. They would move in together and all would be right with the world. But it just wasn't happening. Time for a plan B.

Before he knew it, the announcement for the Bellingham station had sounded, and he gathered his gear and left the train. A half-hour later he was at the bike owner's house, and the bike was cleaned and parked in front, as perfect as Shane had imagined it. It had an after-market exhaust system that gave the bike a much more manly sound than the stock exhaust. He loved it. The tires and brakes were in decent shape. He gave it a test ride and, after a brief negotiation, they settled on a price. He pulled out his jacket, torso protector vest, and helmet, strapped on the backpack that he had carried everything in, and headed out down the road.

He could feel the power of the bike underneath him. The new fuel injection system gave it an almost instant surge when he hit the throttle. Instead of taking the boring I5 highway back home, he decided to turn off toward Whidbey Island, a thirty-mile-long, banana-shaped island north of Seattle. It was accessible by a beautiful bridge on the north end, and a ferry ride on the south end. As he neared the island, the road became narrow, winding its path through beautiful evergreen trees. He leaned into the turns, becoming more confident with every mile. He opened up the bike when he came to a long stretch, and within seconds he looked down and realized he had crossed one hundred miles an hour. He immediately slowed down, a bit shaken by his inability to recognize how fast he was going. But a surge of pride went through him; he had hit one hundred miles an hour on a motorcycle! That was certainly one for his personal record books. It was a glorious day.

The bike was spectacular. Crazy fast, no windshield or fairings to get in the way. Just the wind in his face and power on demand.

He had never felt so alive. He reached the Deception Pass bridge on the north side of Whidbey Island. The narrow bridge rose elegantly four or five hundred feet above the narrow pass. Going across it on the bike sent a chill up his spine. Soon he was past Oak Harbor and on the open road, heading south through the heart of the island.

He was cruising along without a care in the world when he came up behind a long line of cars. He slowed down to close to 40 miles per hour. The speed limit was fifty-five, but there was no room to pass. There were six or seven cars in front of him, and cars coming intermittently from the other direction on the two-lane road. At first he thought it would be too dangerous to pass, but within minutes he was frustrated by the ridiculously slow speed.

Then he noticed the woman driving the large car just ahead of him. She was swerving as she appeared to be trying to put on her makeup using the rearview mirror. A little girl played in the passenger seat, tugging at the woman's arm and obviously annoying her. It was clear to Shane that she was not concerned with her driving, but rather with the activities inside her car.

The plodding convoy came around a curve and there was an opening, and Shane went for it. By the time he passed the last car he was doing over ninety miles an hour, and he darted back into his own lane shortly before another car coming from the other direction passed by.

He looked in his rearview mirror and went from absolute exhilaration to stunned terror. There was a collision just behind him. He slowed and made a quick U-turn toward the accident. One car had gone into the ditch and hit a telephone pole. The other had flipped upside down with its wheels still rolling, a hundred feet from the car in the ditch. The car in the ditch had its hood popped up. Its engine was on fire, and flames were already lapping up the telephone pole. Shane parked the bike and ran down into the ditch. After several tries he was able to yank the door open. A groggy little girl was pulling on her limp mother as flames started to flicker from under the dashboard.

Shane grabbed the girl without thinking, and pulled her out kicking and screaming, "Help my mommy! Help my mommy!" He quickly carried the girl twenty feet up the bank to the side of the road and pushed her into the arms of a female spectator, yelling, "Don't let go of her!"

He then bolted back down to the car, fighting through flames at this point, the dried grass and undercarriage of the car completely engulfed. He dove headfirst into the passenger side, grabbed the woman, and pulled as hard as he could. With one great lunge, they both fell backward out of the car. Shane landed on his back, onto a bed of burning grass, the woman landing directly on top of him, partially knocking the wind out of him. He got to his feet, gasping for breath, and started dragging the woman away. Another man showed up, and together they were able to get her away from the flames, dragging and pulling her up the ditch's steep banks to the side of the road.

At this point the gas tank lit and the car exploded. They moved the woman to the other side of the street as the flames intensified. Away from the heat, Shane sat back on the road, gasping for breath as other people began to help the woman.

Panicked voices came to him through the hectic scene. "Don't move her, don't move her!" someone said, and Shane actually laughed. In a blur, he looked around as ambulances and fire trucks quickly arrived, the paramedics yelling for people to give them room. Overhead, a plane circled. One of the firemen had a Jaws of Life in his arms as he rushed toward the upside-down car. Shane had no idea how long he had been sitting there at the side of the road. He got up, walked back to his bike, started it up, and headed down the road.

The air rushing by him felt good, the best cooling sensation he had ever felt in his life in fact. He was still processing what had happened, wondering if it had been a dream. He calmly cruised along, looking at the trees as they flew by him in a surreal blur.

He then glanced at his gloves and started to feel the pain. They seemed to be partially melted, and his jacket was in tatters. He smelled burned rubber and initially thought it was lingering from the accident, then realized that it was his clothes.

It was not a dream.

He was not sure how far he had ridden when he saw a sign for a twenty-four hour emergency clinic and pulled into the lot. He got off of the bike and staggered through the front door.

At the reception desk were two girls, apparently twins. They had their heads buried in a magazine, completely ignoring the fact that he had just walked in. A moment later a woman in a white coat and a head scarf came in from a side door. She started to give some instructions to the girls, then looked at Shane and said, "Oh my God!"

At this point both girls looked up and gasped. He looked from the girls to the woman as they stared at him. He was able to force his helmet's face shield open and said, "Can I get some help, please?"

The woman in the white coat quickly set her clipboard down and rushed to him. "Is your head injured? Do you feel any neck pain?"

He shook his head. "I'm a little confused, but there's no pain in my head or neck."

She undid the helmet strap and slowly worked his helmet off. "Come on then," she said, leading him by his arm to the first treatment room and sitting him in the chair. "I need to get some things, don't move," she said firmly.

"No plans to move, no worries," he said with a smile. She gave him a smirk that he found very pleasant.

Moments later the doctor came back into the room with a tray full of instruments, the girls from the front desk right behind her.

"Sasha, get some gauze pads and some wraps and tape. Savanna, help me here."

She started systematically working her way from Shane's head downwards, asking questions as she went. His head and neck seemed fine; his helmet, however, looked like someone had taken a blow torch to it. There seemed to be some tenderness in his abdomen.

"Well, it looks like your helmet saved you from some nasty burns and scars. What in the world happened to you?" the doctor asked.

"Just another pulling-mom-and-daughter-out-of-burning-car type thing," Shane joked. "It happens all the time. I was just heading home to Ballard when it all happened."

The doctor gave a short laugh and looked more closely at his gloved hands. "OK, we are going to have to cut and scrape these gloves off. Apparently, they were not made for fire protection. I will need to give you some anesthetic."

Shane said, "I'll be OK. I've got a fairly high pain tolerance most times, but I'll concede it does sting a bit."

"Trust me on this one, I'm giving you anesthetic whether you want it or not," said the doctor firmly.

"OK, you're the boss. Could you tell me your name before the torture treatment?" Shane said, smiling.

She responded with a smirk again; he was becoming quite enamored with the smirk. After a few pokes of anesthetic, she raised her eyes without lifting her head, then looked back down. "I'm Emma. My daughters are Sasha and Savanna."

"Nice to meet you. I'm Shane," he said with a yelp as she pulled a piece of glove away.

"Let's give the anesthetic a little more time," she said. Shane nodded in agreement, gritting his teeth.

An hour later the gloves had been extracted from his hands, which were professionally bandaged. He had a couple of codeine pills in him at this point and wasn't feeling half bad, until he tried to stand.

Emma noticed his groan and said, "OK, problem B, what is happening?"

"I don't know, it just seems like something is out of sorts down there, just around my pubic hair line."

"OK, well you're going to have to drop your drawers and let me take a look."

Shane stood, but was unable to undo his belt with his bandaged hands so Emma took over. "I need to take your pants down to see what is going on," she said.

"Well, no woman has ever said it quite that way, but yes, I'm OK with you taking my pants off."

Emma glanced up angrily. "Sorry," Shane said. "Just trying to keep the situation light. Yes you have permission, thank you for asking."

She lowered his pants and they both saw a lump the size of a large walnut just above the pubic hair line. "Ok, I'm going to put my hand on it. When I do, bear down a little as if tightening your stomach, or cough a bit, your choice," said Emma.

Shane did it and immediately Emma said "You have a fairly significant hernia. I do not believe it is an emergency, but you will need surgery as soon as possible to fix it."

Shane replied, "Well, she was a fairly large woman that I pulled out of the burning car, unless the whole thing was a dream."

Emma's smirk softened to a partial smile. "Based on the torched helmet, glued-on gloves, and nasty hernia, I can assure you that whatever happened was not a dream." She looked again at the hernia. "Listen, my daughters are going to be in pre-med starting Monday. I would like them to look at this, do you mind if I bring them in briefly? I've been doing this for some time, and I've never seen a hernia so obvious."

Shane felt himself blush. "Uhhh... yeah, well, I... sure, OK. As long as it's brief and in-the-name-of-science type thing... can I pull my underwear up so it covers my privates, at least?"

She gave a short laugh. "Yes, that would be fine."

"Could you help me up with my drawers?"

She smiled with pursed lips as she reached down and lifted Shane's shorts just above his penis, leaving the hernia exposed. "Does this work?"

Shane looked down. "Yes... can we do this fairly quickly?"

"Of course." She smiled and left the room. A short time later there was a light knock and the three women entered.

"OK girls, this is going to be quick," Emma said. "The patient came in with obvious injuries, and complaining of lower abdominal pain. Patient described lifting a heavy object during a time of great duress and stress, meaning he could have lifted more weight than he normally would have been able to. Any guess as to what the problem might be?"

The girls stared at her blankly.

She sighed. "He has a hernia, which is a tear in the intestinal wall. In men it usually occurs right down here, only not so obvious." She pointed to the lump, which immediately elicited an "eww" from both girls at the same time.

"Eww?" Shane said, somewhat sarcastically. Smirk.

"Look girls, you start medical school Monday," Emma said. "It is time to start acting a little more adult and taking things a little more seriously. There is more to life than sitting around reading trashy magazines and playing your Fuqau game. If you don't start acting like you want to do this, I'm not going to keep working at this awful clinic to put you girls through school."

She turned to Shane and said sheepishly, "Sorry, that was unprofessional."

He smiled at her. "No worries. So are we done here?"

"No!" she said abruptly, then softened and said "no, please wait a moment more."

"Sasha, let me show you." Emma grabbed Sasha's hand and slowly moved it down. A silent, extended "ewww" came out of Sasha's mouth as her fingers met the protrusion.

"OK, Shane, if you would bear down as before." As he did, Sasha let out a yelp, and said, "Oh my God, it feels like an alien in there."

"Thanks," Shane said derisively.

"Oooh, let me feel, let me feel," said Savanna. She didn't need her mother's help, but reached down and felt it, then said, "OK, Mister, please bear down for me." Shane bore down as she held her hand on the protrusion, then said "wow, that is freaking amazing. Oh look, does it make that move too, when you bear down?" She pointed to the bulge in his underwear, which was starting to move.

"That's it! Everyone out!!" burst out Shane.

"Savanna, you don't say something like that!" Emma said furiously.

"Out! Out! Out!" said Shane, pointing to the door, and the three women quickly exited.

Shane just stood there a moment, absorbing what had just happened. What a weird freaking day. He was back to thinking it must all be a dream, but the pain in his hands and groin was real. He stood there for a bit, regaining his composure, then reached down and with great effort was able to get his pants up when he heard a knock.

"Shane, can I come in please?" Emma's voice came through the door.

"Not yet, give me a moment." After fighting with his pants for a bit longer and not being able to button them or get the belt fixed, he said, "I need a little help in here. Just you, please, if you would."

She came in and shut the door behind her. She did not meet his eyes, just gently buttoned his pants and fixed his belt, then sat in the chair in the corner, head down.

"Look, this has been the craziest day in a long time," she began.

"Tell me about it." He chuckled.

"What I'm trying to say is that what happened a few minutes ago was inappropriate and irresponsible and unprofessional, and I'm very embarrassed. It's been a rough go getting the girls to this point, and I need to keep this job. I would appreciate it if you kept this between us."

Shane rolled his eyes, blowing out a breath. She waited. "I'm not going to say anything. You seem to be a competent doctor. I am very grateful that you are the one that I stumbled upon. I'm just not sure the girls are cut out for medical work."

Her smirk softened into a smile, and she looked into his eyes. "Thank you, that was very sweet."

They sat there for a few moments just looking at each other. He felt very comfortable around her, despite the disastrous examination.

Shane then said, "Well, I guess I should be going."

Emma brought him to reality. "Not to point out the obvious, but you're fifty miles and a ferry ride away from Ballard, you have a melted helmet, two extremely bandaged hands and an alien coming out of your stomach. I don't think you'll be riding anywhere today."

Shane thought for a moment. "Good point. I'll have to get a taxi."

Emma felt an odd connection to this man as a chill ran through her. There was something about him that seemed familiar; somehow she knew him. One thing she knew for sure was that he was injured enough that he should not be alone.

"Listen, my shift is over shortly. Why don't you come home with us? We have a comfortable couch. We will pamper you a bit and feed you dinner and breakfast, then take you back to Seattle in the morning. It's Friday, and I don't work again until Wednesday. This would be easy."

He looked startled, then gave her a cautious smile. "That's a very generous offer. But you must let me pay you back. I will agree to stay with you tonight if you and the girls agree to be guests at my house for the weekend—I have a vacation rental unit upstairs, and no guests this weekend. If they are starting school on Monday, it would be perfect. I'm just a mile or so from the university, and you'll have the whole upper part of the house to yourselves."

"Well, as far as professional standards go, I'm so far past any degree of normalcy at this point that we might as well. Let me check with the girls." Emma felt herself smiling as she left the room.

CHAPTER THIRTY-FOUR

Once they all agreed to the plan, they managed to push Shane's bike around to the back of the building and they all loaded into Emma's car. The girls were a bit taken aback when told they would be having an evening guest, but warmed to the idea when they saw how happy their mother was. Their routine for security of no guests had made all of them very introverted.

On the drive home, the girls bickered and laughed while showing each other various things in the gossip magazines they had brought with them, until Emma said, "Girls, can you give the magazines a break for a bit?"

They both groaned but put the magazines down and stared out the windows, pouting. Shane thought that it was interesting that they acted almost in unison, and he found their behavior immature, yet somehow charming.

Sasha said something to Savanna in a language that sounded Middle Eastern to Shane. "English, please," said Emma.

"It's OK, really," said Shane, "what is that, Arabic or something?"

The look on Emma's face indicated he had just said something really stupid.

"No Shane, not Arabic. It is Persian. We are from Iran," said Emma.

"I'll be honest, I didn't know there was a difference, I thought it was all Ara..." He trailed off mid-sentence, realizing too late that it was another stupid thing to say.

Emma chucked. "It's OK, Shane. Ignorance of the Iranian culture is pretty widespread in this country; it's not just you."

Emma had rented a house right on the water near a little town on the south end of the island, very isolated and with spectacular views. It was set back from the main road a few hundred feet, and the driveway was lined with beautiful evergreen trees. Probably second growth, Shane thought, but beautiful trees anyway. As they pulled up to the home he could see the well-manicured yard. Steps leading to the front door were lined with lovely planter boxes of flowers—perhaps not as vibrant as possible, as the huge trees fought for most of the sunlight on that side of the house—but lovely just the same.

Emma parked the car and they went inside. The home was simple but meticulously clean, with comfortable furniture and striking artwork. There were many apparently African items around, a combination of clever carvings, weavings, a few paintings, and chairs that looked like they were carved out of a single piece of wood. The colors in the room were stunning.

"I take it you have an interest in Africa?" Shane said, as Emma was putting away her things.

"Yes, very much. I spent two years there in a few clinics in the middle of nowhere, just before coming back here. There is a lot of beauty in Africa."

"Wow, that's impressive. It must be a bit of a shock to be working at a clinic on Whidbey Island." Shane immediately regretted the words, thinking he sounded a bit snarky.

To his relief, Emma laughed. "Culture shock it is, but it pays the bills, and I'm just not interested in working at a major hospital or getting back into private practice. Both of those can be debilitating and impossible to escape from."

"I didn't mean to sound demeaning," Shane said hastily. "It's just that for some people, working in Africa would be a dream job. Why did you come back?"

Emma led the way to the kitchen at the back of the house. "Our situation is a bit complicated, but ultimately we came home primarily for the girls. I home-schooled them there, and I'm really not that good of a teacher. Fortunately, many smart young people came through the clinics as volunteers, people from all over the world, and they would help with the home-school classes. So I think they actually got a pretty good education. As to their personal development, there wasn't much in the way of social interaction. So when the clinic job offer came up, it was kind of a family decision. It's worked out, for the most part. They were both accepted at the University of Washington's medical school, which I'm thankful for. I've got some money, but medical school for two girls can be pricey. I think we'll get through this."

Shane was listening intently, wondering where the girls' father might be in this picture. He didn't ask, but said, "I think they might not appreciate it now, but when they're our age they might feel differently. Traveling is such a great experience."

Laughing, Emma said, "Yes. They weren't exactly thrilled when they saw their first squat toilet in Africa, but we all adjusted, and I think we're all better for it. I hope to go back again after they get through school. The people there are beautiful—it is just the politics that are messed up." She opened a bottle of red wine, poured them each a glass, and started preparing dinner.

Shane was standing near the counter trying to find the right way to ask. He finally blurted, "So why are you Persian if you're from Iran? Wouldn't that make you Iranian?"

Emma looked at him and gave a big sigh. "We are from Iran, yes, but Persian is what we consider ourselves."

Shane thought a moment. He was almost sure there wasn't a country called Persia. Were people from Saudi Arabia the Arabic ones? That didn't seem like a smart question, so he went with his first thought. "So, is Persia part of the Middle East?"

Emma's expression gave Shane the clear impression that he had just said something really stupid. "No Shane, there is not a country called Persia, at least not in modern times. Our family is mostly from Iran, but we consider ourselves Persian. Most people who don't necessarily associate with the Iranian regime, but who are from that area, will describe themselves by ethnicity instead of nationality. Although, even that isn't quite right." She went back to chopping onions then added, "People in the US don't exactly greet you with open arms when you say you are Iranian. They instantly associate you with terrorists."

"Huh," said Shane, desperately trying to think something smart to say. "And the head scarf, is that Persian?"

Again, Emma gave him the look. "I am Muslim. I voluntarily became one, and when I married my husband, we started out very religious. I'm glad I did, although at this point I've lost so much of it that I'm barely hanging on to any part of it, I admit. The scarf is my version of a hijab, which is basically a head covering meant to show modesty. As a Muslim, modesty and morality are at the core. You must not walk around looking like a temptress or whore."

Shane hesitated, then said "Well, I wouldn't have thought that about you, even without the head scarf." At Emma's glowing smile, Shane felt proud of himself for seemingly saying the right thing.

The girls were planted comfortably at opposite ends of the couch reading, but both listening in on the conversation when Savanna said, "I don't know why you still wear the hijab, mother. It would be so much easier to integrate here if you dumped it."

"I wear it out of respect for your father," Emma said firmly. "There are many good things about Islam, and I fear that the two of you have fallen so far away from it that you will never understand your roots."

Savanna shot back, "You do a bunch of other things that aren't Islamic, like alcohol, for one."

Emma gave her an angry stare from across the room, then picked up the wine bottle. She refilled the glasses and said, "Yes, it is one of the things that I appreciate about Christianity."

Shane burst out laughing. The girls joined in, chuckling more at his response than at what their mother had said.

Emma murmured, "I do worry about future generations."

"We heard that, mother," said Sasha.

"Good, it was meant to be heard." Emma chuckled under her breath.

She finished putting together the salad and pulled some chicken breasts out of the fridge. She and Shane headed out to the deck, fired up the grill and laid out the chicken breasts.

The chicken looked like it had been marinating all day, and Shane thought it all looked delicious. He was starving at this point; it had been quite a day and he was just realizing that he hadn't eaten much.

He and Emma settled into the deck chairs and looked out on the bay. It was a beautiful evening, still close to eighty degrees, with not a cloud in the sky—something rare in the Seattle area, and to be appreciated.

They sat there for a few minutes sipping the wine as they watched the occasional boat meander by. Emma then asked, "So what is the whole story? What happened today?"

Shane took a big drink of wine and motioned for more. She filled his glass, smiling. "Well, the short version is that I took the train this morning up to Bellingham to pick up that bike, and decided to come back through Whidbey Island instead of the I-5.

I got stuck behind a line of cars, just north of Coupeville, it must have been. I passed them, then I looked in my mirror and saw an accident behind me. Come to think of it, it was that idiot woman just ahead of me; she must have followed me while I was passing and hit the car coming from the other direction. I feel sorry for the little girl, but she seemed OK. Not sure about the mom."

"They must have taken them all to the hospital at Coupeville," Emma said. "They have a decent emergency room there, as it covers the whole island. It must have been crazy at the scene, though."

"Yeah, it's all kind of fuzzy, but basically, I ran down to the car and grabbed the girl, and another fellow helped me with the woman. Man, that was a big woman." It was coming back to him now. "The car exploded when we were about twenty feet from it. If we had been any later, that lady would have been toast." He smiled. "Sorry for the expression."

Emma laughed.

"Before I knew it, ambulances and fire trucks were everywhere. They were mostly concerned for the woman and the occupants of the other car." He looked out at the water, remembering the car upturned in the ditch. "I'm guessing things didn't turn out too well with the other folks. I just hope they survived. I got back on my bike and headed down the road. I really don't know how long it was before I realized I was burned. The air flowing over me felt great and I was just kind of ignoring the pain, I think."

"Most likely you were in shock. That is quite a story."

Shane went on, "Once I realized I was hurt, I looked up and saw your sign, walked in, then you all looked at me and screamed, and the rest you know."

Emma laughed. She was charmed by the way he underestimated his role in the whole thing. A man who could handle pain without whimpering, and who could do the right thing without thinking, was admirable. She had been around enough men in her life who didn't possess either of these traits. She knew what she liked, and she liked this guy sharing a glass of wine with her with his two bandaged hands awkwardly holding the glass. If he was in pain, which he must have been, he wasn't showing it.

She was looking at him glowingly when he turned to her, looked right in her eyes and said, "I think the chicken is burning."

Emma yelped and stood up quickly, spilling her wine. She rushed to the BBQ, turned over the chicken and groaned. "Well, blackened chicken is a specialty of mine, just so you know."

Shane laughed. "That's one of my favorite foods, no worries."

It wasn't one of the girls' favorite foods. They sat at the table, complaining about the chicken. "Oh, for Christ's sake, just peel off the skin and eat the chicken," said Emma. "You know how it was in Africa. This would have been appreciated by many a person there."

With that, both girls looked a little sheepish, and Savanna said, "Yeah, sorry," and started fixing the chicken to her liking.

The story of the crash and burning car was repeated for the girls, with more details as Shane's memory of it became clearer. The girls were clearly amazed.

Sasha asked, "What happened to the little girl? Was she hurt?"

"I don't know," Shane said, "but she was in good hands the last time I saw her. I'm pretty sure she was OK. The mother was partially conscious when I left, but she seemed to be coming around, and the paramedics had taken control. As for the folks in the other car, I fear the worst, unfortunately, but the ambulances and fire trucks were all there very quickly. I'm not sure where it happened, to be honest, but it must have been near Coupeville... in fact it was, I remember now... that walking bridge that goes across the main road as you're going by the town... there were a bunch of people up there on it, watching what was going on. I was in kind of a cloud there for a bit."

Both girls were looking at him with what looked like glowing adoration. Noticing this, Emma decided to change the subject. "So anyway," she told the girls. "Tomorrow we are going to go to

Ballard and stay in Shane's guesthouse for the weekend, and on Monday we'll go to the university. I'm going to find a new car this weekend for myself, and you girls will have the Mazda to use."

With that, both girls squealed with delight. The car was unexpected. "You'll need to figure out a car parking pass," Emma continued. "Just let me know the cost and I'll pay for it. The car is to be SHARED, and I expect you two to work it out. NO ACCIDENTS. Drive like you have a baby in the car with you at all times. UNDERSTOOD?" She eyed them fiercely.

Simultaneously, they both said "understood," unable to hide their excitement. Shane snickered, thinking that they were a very charming little family.

After dinner and the bottle of wine, Shane was done, and Emma could see it.

"Are you OK with sleeping on a couch?" she asked.

"Absolutely, I'll be out like a light as soon as my head hits the armrest."

She got out some sheets and set him up. "The bathroom is the first door on the left. A bath might be easier with your hands; do you want me to get a tub ready?"

Without hesitating, Shane said, "That would be fabulous, I thought you'd never ask." He smiled.

In the bath, Shane was able to get himself reasonably clean without getting his bandages wet. Emma had left him a large bathrobe; he decided he was not going to ask whose it was. He made his way back into the living room and crawled under the sheets. He was feeling great—she had given him codeine, which had dulled most of the throbbing in his body. Before he knew it, he was sound asleep.

Emma returned shortly afterward to say goodnight, realized he was already asleep, smiled and tucked the blanket over him. She looked at him for a few seconds longer, wondering what had just crashed into her life. That seemed to be how it happened for her, but she did not want to think about it or hope for something that wasn't there. The next few days, if nothing else, were bound to be interesting.

The girls went to their room very excited about the day. As was their habit, they shifted into speaking Fuqua, which was a made-up term for the way they spoke to each other when alone. It had started out as a game many years before, and they had gotten so used to speaking it that they would often slip into Fuqua when their mother was around, much to Emma's annoyance. But she found it so impressive that she could not get too angry.

When the girls were growing up, as they moved from country to country following their mother's clinic stints, they were able to immerse themselves in the local language, and it was a race to see who could become fluent first. The idea with Fuqua was to shift from language to language: when one spoke, the other had to respond in another language, then the response had to be a third language, then another, etc. The girls now fluently spoke French, English, Persian, German, and Dutch. This combination of languages allowed them to converse almost anywhere they went. When they spoke Fuqua, the five languages would flow from one to another seamlessly. It was bizarre to listen to when they were in full Fuqua, but they were able to do it with ease.

They also enjoyed the stunned looks on peoples' faces. The trick was to shift out of it when talking with someone other than each other.

Not only were the twins physically beautiful, but by the time they returned to the US for their final year of high school, they were leap years ahead of the other students, academically at least.

They mostly kept to themselves, as the jealousy and torment from the other girls was awful. The boys were all idiots from their perspective. It seemed like most of the kids couldn't even speak English correctly, and their complete lack of understanding of other cultures and lack of international exposure made them so uninteresting to the twins that the two girls came off as stuck up, which they certainly didn't mean to be. Their own superiority made the year miserable, and they couldn't wait to get home each day.

Years of isolation and being immersed in a world where their other friends were primarily brilliant college-age interns, made both girls yearn to get to the next stage of their lives. But Emma was very clear that they needed to do their best for their final year of high school, and that they would have to make it work somehow.

That night, as the girls closed their bedroom door, the Fuqua kicked in. Sasha began in English. "I can hardly believe this day. That was a pretty amazing thing that happened to Shane."

Savanna responded in Persian. "Yes, and he is quite a beautiful man as well."

Sasha replied in flawless French, "Forget it! You are much too ugly for him."

Savanna shot back in Dutch, "You forget we are identical twins! So you must be ugly too."

Sasha finished in German. "Well, at least we both look more like mom than dad," which had them both laughing.

They had some old pictures of their dad, a couple from when they were just babies, on one of the family's infrequent beach vacations. He was slim, dark and very handsome, and also very hairy. The girls had inherited all of their mother's beauty and then some, and they were both appreciative of that. But they really didn't have any idea how beautiful they truly were.

Downstairs, Emma got ready for bed, worrying about what her dreams would be like tonight. The dreams, which she'd begun having after Hamid's death, were becoming more intense recently. In the dreams they would be walking together on a path, on a beautiful fall day, with the leaves falling all around them, and lying in soft piles under their feet. It was a beautiful path, with light at the end, and light and trees and safety surrounding them. The walk was gently endless, and they were together with nothing else in the world but each other. The path wandered ahead with no destination, no expectation; it was just a path. In other dreams, she and Hamid would be sitting and drinking tea together.

She usually looked forward to going to sleep at night, because Hamid would always be there with her. Even after all these years, the dreams came. There were times when she thought she could feel his hand holding hers, even squeezing it. Sometimes the dreams were so vivid that when she woke she would look over at the pillow beside her, almost expecting him to be there.

Lately, though, something had changed, and it was disturbing her. Hamid seemed to not be walking right in the dreams. He was dragging his feet like he couldn't walk or was very tired. He looked old.

She had been doing a lot of reflecting recently and decided that the dreams must stop, that she must move on. The girls were soon off to college, and she would be alone, and she did not want to live that way for the rest of her life. She wanted to have a partner, and she knew that Hamid would understand. She was sure these thoughts were contributing to the change in her dreams.

So tonight she decided that she would just make the dreams stop, that she was moving on. She told herself that over and over before going to sleep, commanding her mind to break away, to let go...

That night, for the first time in 16 years, Hamid spoke to her.

CHAPTER THIRTY-FIVE

"I am dying."

Emma bolted upright in bed, stunned awake, frantically looking around at the darkness surrounding her. Her heart was beating too fast; she couldn't breathe. She rocked back and forth, holding a pillow in front of her, terrified. Hamid had never spoken to her in a dream in sixteen years, now he told her he was dying? The dream made no sense.

She was shaking with fear and desperate grief as she cried uncontrollably. She rolled out of bed and onto the floor, crawling madly around room, her breath coming in frantic gasps. "Oh my God, oh my God, oh my God." She crawled into the bathroom, reached up and turned on the shower, and pulled herself under the cold water with her pajamas still on. She had lost all sense of where she was and what she was doing—her brain felt like it was on fire as the cold water poured over her. She soon began to shiver and started to come out of the shock of the dream.

She pulled herself up and turned off the water, and crumpled back down to the floor, crying and gulping air. She stayed there, slumped in the shower stall, until the cold became unbearable. She forced herself to stand and was able to get out of her wet clothes. She got back into bed with her eyes wide open, her mind still ablaze and racing for answers that were not there.

CHAPTER THIRTY-SIX

The next morning, Shane rose early. He could smell the aroma of a coffee found only in the Northwest—he loved that part of living in Seattle. He organized the couch bedding as best he could with his bandaged hands, and went into the kitchen. "Good morning," he said, noticing the worn look on Emma's face. "Looks like someone didn't sleep much last night."

She just gave him an exhausted nod, and unceremoniously handed him his coffee. They both walked out onto the deck and settled in to watch the sun rise above the tree line across the inlet. The morning quickly warmed, as it promised to be an eighty-degree day. The coffee was as good as it got, a finely ground espresso blend with a creamy coffee head and a wonderful aroma. Even before Shane took a sip he was looking forward to his second cup.

The girls were not exactly early risers. Emma explained that it might be an hour or so before they all headed out, as it was not easy getting them moving, and on the weekends she would take a break from being the pushy mom and let them sleep in a bit.

This was fine by Shane. His feet were kicked up on the stool in front of him and he was able to hold his coffee cup with his bandaged hand. As long as he didn't move much, his gut didn't hurt. It was a beautiful sunrise and a gorgeous woman was doting over him. Life just didn't get any better. They sat silently together for a good while, Emma appreciating the calm and quiet but also appreciating the company. Even though they were so different, it was good to have a man next to her.

"So, I'm curious about many aspects of your life, but not sure where to begin," Shane said.

Emma sighed, wanting to move on from the dream. "Well, it's been mostly a blur at times, a nightmare at other times."

Shane laughed. "It couldn't be that bad! It seems like you've got a pretty good thing going, and your daughters seem amazing. I can't tell Sasha from Savanna yet, by the way. What was the language that one of them spoke?"

"Well, that was Persian earlier, but they also speak French, German, and Dutch, all fluently, way beyond my capabilities."

"Lord, you have got to be kidding me! How did that happen?"

Emma took a sip of coffee. "It was all from our travels. Once I returned from Iran, I worked briefly in Seattle as general practitioner specializing in women's health, then I hooked up with a global institute. They would send me all over the world, mostly to third world countries, to set up and manage clinics. I think we did a lot of good, but it was depressing because the need was so great and we could only do so much. We had terrific resources and access to the latest medicine, but sick and pregnant women had to get there. We would have pregnant mothers with five children in tow walking a hundred miles to get help. It was heartbreaking and it was every day—a big reality check. I became an expert at fixing fistula, even though I wasn't a surgeon."

"Fistula?" Shane asked.

"Yeah, that is a particularly nasty problem in Africa. Usually it appears in pregnant girls who are too young to be having babies—they get a tear or hole in their bowels or urinary tract during childbirth, and feces and urine leak out. There's no way to stop it without surgery. It is a fairly minor surgery, but there just aren't enough qualified surgeons. Young women become lepers in their community because they smell so bad. It is tragic."

Shane was stunned. "Yikes... I've been living a fairly isolated life. I had no idea this even happened in the world."

Emma nodded. "Well, you steel yourself to it, keep telling yourself how much good you are doing and how this person is now alive because of you and can integrate back into the community, and maybe they will be the next great leader of their country because of what you are doing—that type of thinking gets you through it. But there are so many that don't get help, that is the tragic part. My last stint in Africa was the hardest; the governments there take nepotism and corruption to a new level. There is nothing like a generation of colonial rule to completely screw up a continent."

"Humph," Shane said. "I hadn't really given Africa much thought until now. I mean, I knew there were problems but it just wasn't on my radar."

They stopped talking for a moment, Shane thinking about the right way to change the subject. "So I'm curious, Emma. What about your ex-husband? Is he Iranian? I mean, Persian?" This prompted another audible sigh from Emma.

"He's not my ex-husband. I'm not divorced, I'm a widow. But to answer your question, yes, he was from Iran. Just so you know, I'm half Iranian too, on my mother's side." She took a sip of coffee and looked across the water, not making eye contact with Shane.

"I was always attracted to Iranian men, for some reason," she continued. "Physically and culturally. But normally their misogynistic tendencies would drive me mad. But my husband was truly different. We met at the university when he was an exchange student studying pre-med, and we married while in school and had the twins shortly after graduation. He wanted to return to Iran, telling me how beautiful it was and how great the people were, but I was hesitant, because it was a war zone. Long story, but women don't have a lot of rights in Iran these days. It can be a difficult place if you're not a male, especially if you have grown up in a western society. Also, he had switched to nuclear engineering, and there were a lot of questions being asked from government people here about an Iranian national with a nuclear degree. We made a family decision that it was probably best to leave the United States."

"Questions about what?" asked Shane.

"They were mostly concerned he was going to go back to Iran and build a bomb. He would never do that—he was not interested in destruction—but they didn't seem to believe him. We left quickly because we thought that they might put him in jail, we just didn't know."

"Huh," said Shane. "So what was it like when you got there?"

"It really wasn't bad. The family connections were wonderful, the food, the culture. The people are beautiful and loving, but when men rule every aspect of society, well, that tends to not be a great thing. The old saying of 'absolute power corrupts absolutely' applies there, and although many men are good and loving and pious and everything, there are evil ones as well."

"But that is true everywhere, isn't it?" Shane said.

Emma nodded. "My husband was very special, though. He was a loving, kind man, and also very loyal to Iran. When the call came shortly after we arrived to help out in the war with Iraq, he went. His English and technical skills were greatly needed—there weren't exactly any Americans around to help out with all of the war machines that the Shah had purchased. He was sure he would just be in a support role, helping train people to use all of the American equipment that was still functional. They were short on spare parts and expertise; most of them couldn't even understand the manuals or how to operate things, so he was quickly a head trainer for technical and repair work, and spent a lot of his time just translating things into Persian. He made it clear he would not get involved in the nuclear program. Regardless, he moved up to a fairly high place of authority in the Republican Guard. That was never his goal, he was just smart. He never really trusted them either—he considered himself Persian and was extremely loyal to his roots. The regime made him uncomfortable, but his loyalty never wavered. He wanted to save his country."

She took another sip of coffee and continued.

"I was never told how it happened. I got a letter saying he was dead, killed somehow in the war, and I came back here to the States with the girls, then traveled with work for years. He was a good man; I have a lot of respect for him and always will. I was deeply in love with him."

Shane thought for a moment. "Was it easy to get out of Iran?"

Emma laughed. "Not exactly. But getting out is a story for another time."

By now Shane's coffee was empty. He looked at it, then looked at Emma, who seemed lost in thought. He then started to awkwardly stand and move towards the kitchen.

Emma said, "Let me guess: after that story you don't want to feel like you are being too demanding and are going to get yourself your own cup of coffee?"

Shane looked at her, not sure how to respond. "Well, yeah, I guess."

Emma laughed, hopped up and grabbed the cup out of his hand, and went back into the kitchen.

Shane watched her as she moved back inside. She was lovely. Whip smart, worldly, exotic—he was sure she was the most attractive woman he had ever met, and she was making him coffee first thing in the morning after healing him, and he was now about to spend the rest of the weekend with her. The girls would be with them for the next couple of days, but it promised to be an interesting weekend anyway, and he hadn't had a lot of those recently.

Emma handed him his new coffee, sat back down and looked across the water as the sun was rising above the trees.

"I have dreamed about my husband every night since he died," she said.

Shane looked at her. "What?"

"For sixteen years, every night in my dreams we go for a walk," she said. "It is on a path, through trees, there is light at the end, the path is covered with soft leaves. We never talk; we just walk on the path together. It is beautiful, safe, quiet. Sometimes we sit and have tea. It is a similar dream every night. There are times where I feel like I am losing my mind." Emma paused, taking a sip of coffee.

"Dreams are a strange thing," she continued. "I know he is dead, but I still feel him. At first I resisted the dreams, trying to force him out of my mind because the grief was so strong. Eventually I learned to accept the dreams. The only thing that is different in the dreams is that sometimes he is holding my hand tighter than other times. I don't understand the significance of that. I spent thousands of dollars on therapy and astrology and hypnosis and have tried everything I can think of, but nothing changes."

Emma fell silent. After a moment she said, "I shouldn't have told you this; it is not your concern."

Shane thought for a moment, staring out at the water. "I'm glad you told me. I have never heard of such a thing."

Emma found his honesty and straightforwardness refreshing. It was good to have an adult to talk to who was not a therapist, even if the two of them seemed to be polar opposites.

"It just makes it difficult to be with another man," she said. "You can't exactly tell a man you're dating that you dream about someone else every night. Not a real relationship builder."

Shane chuckled. "Yeah, you're right about that. But remember also that most American men are pretty simple-minded when it comes to sex. As long as I'm the one getting laid, I couldn't care less who the woman is thinking about."

"Oh, yuck!" Emma said laughing, smacking Shane playfully as she stood up.

CHAPTER THIRTY-SEVEN

Soon they were packing the car for the trip to Seattle. The girls had already moved most of their belongings to the dorm room, so they just had the final items to bring. They had protested initially about the dorms, but Emma insisted that they stay there for the first year, hoping that it would help them socialize. Sooner or later, they needed to get out into the real world. That world can be cruel at times, and they might as well learn that lesson early.

The girls had a certain toughness to them, Emma knew, but that side of them had not come out in high school. She felt that it was just a matter of time before they would be asserting themselves.

For now it was one step at a time, and today it was getting the car packed and heading down to Shane's house. They arrived for the nine a.m. ferry crossing to Mukilteo, a short ride and a lovely inlet crossing between Whidbey and the mainland. From there it was a forty-five minute drive to Ballard. It was Saturday, so traffic wasn't too bad, not nearly as bad as a normal weekday commute.

They arrived at Shane's home and pulled into the carport behind his Subaru. Shane had cleaned and readied the house before he left to pick up the motorcycle, in case he got a last-minute booking. He was greatly relieved that the suite was ready; his hands were in no shape to do any cleaning.

His own unit was another story. He had left it kind of a disaster zone, not expecting that anyone would be seeing it anytime soon. As he showed the three women into the upstairs suite, he was strategizing how to manage the weekend without giving them a tour of the whole house. The home had a lovely sweeping view of the valley and Ballard, and the Olympic Mountains to the west were in their full glory.

When they were all settled in, Shane and Emma got back in her car and drove to the car dealership in Ballard. Sasha and Savanna were more than happy to stay home for a soak in the hot tub.

They returned a couple of hours later, Emma following Shane and her coupe in a new Subaru wagon.

On the way home they picked up some fresh salmon from the fish terminal. The Copper River salmon was in season, and was renowned for being the best salmon of the year. The Copper River fish apparently had one of the longest trips salmon take to spawn, requiring lots of fat storage, which made it melt in the mouth. Pricey, but worth it as soon as you took the first bite. They decided to do an afternoon BBQ, giving them time to do something else afterward, if everyone felt motivated to go out for some music or a movie.

They all sat down on the deck for dinner, the girls chatting back and forth in Fuqua as they approached the table. "No more Fuqua," was the stern response from Emma. The girls rolled their eyes.

Shane commented, "I really don't mind, I find it fascinating." He looked at the girls. "It is quite a gift, this little game you girls have created, perhaps unique in the whole world. You really should do a video or something."

"No!" Sasha snapped. Her firmness surprised Shane.

"OK, sorry. Didn't mean anything," he said quickly.

Emma gave Sasha an irritated look. "The Fuqua game has been a very personal thing for them. Whenever they do it in public it just brings too much attention."

To the girls, she said, "But I do think he is right that you should explore it more as you go to school. It is more impressive that either of you know."

Sasha asked, "Can we just eat, already?"

"Fine, ye ole grumpy one," Emma replied.

They sat down and started quietly filling the plates, and as they filled their mouths with the delicious salmon, everyone's mood lightened.

Shane had a perplexed look on his face as he ate his salmon, then said, "I'm still confused over the whole thing—I mean, your history. It sounds I'm not getting the whole story, to be honest."

Emma looked at him and nodded. "Well, we do have a complicated story. Our start in Iran just led to one thing after another, and sometimes life dictates what you do, not the other way around. Iranian culture is complicated because it is thousands of years of society, versus American culture, which is a few hundred. It is all about honor and family, and it is a very patriarchal society. It was evolving to a large degree into a more equal society under the Shah, then the revolution happened. But things weren't perfect under the Shah either. My husband's parents were killed by his secret police."

Shane gave her a shocked look. "Men are the leaders now," she continued, "in the family and politically and religiously. Women are there to serve—that is the way it is for now. The revolution in Iran was a step backward for women, and a step forward for men. This is why I did not want to go back initially, but I went anyway, out of love for my husband. I have no intention of ever being less than equal in a relationship or marriage. It doesn't mean that I don't love Iran and love the people very much, it is just that I have been self-sufficient my whole life, and I want to give my girls every chance to be independent and make up their own minds as adults. Who knows, maybe they will want to go back someday, but they will do that as adults, not as my children."

Shane thought for a moment, then said, "It is confusing for most Americans. I think part of our fear about Arabic people is just not understanding."

Emma shook her head, and said, "Well, lumping us all in as Arabic is the first problem. Iranians who identify as Iranian generally have bought into the revolution, whereas the rest of us consider ourselves Persian. But no Persian or Iranian would ever call themselves Arabic. The Persian language and Arabic language share the same alphabet, but so do Spanish and English, and you can't speak Spanish, I assume?"

Looking a bit sheepish, Shane said, "No, I barely can speak English." He smiled.

Emma went on. "Well, it is the same thing. There are also big differences between Shiite and Sunni—we are all Muslim, but believe in different versions of basically the same thing. Most Arabs are Sunni, most Iranians are Shiite, but not all. There must be dozens of different versions of Islam in Iran alone, and many different languages. It is kind of similar to the Catholics and Protestants battling it out for so many years in England and Ireland: it makes no sense from a distance, but it is what it is. The only problem today is that there are many more radical elements. As a result, honor and family tradition has shifted back into a more traditional version in Iran."

"Dare I ask the differences between a Shiite and Sunni?" asked Shane hesitantly.

Laughing, Emma said, "Well, it goes something like this: when Mohammed died in the seventh century, his successor was disputed. One group wanted it to be a blood lineage, the other wanting the best person for the job. It is a convoluted story from there, but the bottom line is that over the centuries it separated Muslims into two different main sects, both using the Koran, and both having basic similar beliefs. For example, both considered Mohammad to be the last prophet to God, but the big differences of opinion happened once Mohammad died. Today, which shrines are considered the most sacred depends on what you believe... it primarily comes down to how the successor to Mohammad was chosen. There are shrines that are only for Sunnis, and others that are only for Shiites. Usually the shrine is considered the final resting place of one of the descendants or heirs to Mohammad. Mecca in Saudi Arabia is the most famous because it is considered the birthplace of the Prophet Mohammad and it is considered the most sacred spot for both Sunni and Shiites. There are more differences, obviously, but that is kind of the core."

Shane was interested. He never liked coming off as a dumb American, and he was glad to be educated by Emma.

"This is a little off topic," he said. "But I've always been interested in the Iran/Iraq war. It seemed like it was brother fighting brother, from an American perspective." He was doing his best to not sound idiotic.

"Yeah, that is a tough one to explain as well," said Emma. "I had a cousin killed in that war in addition to Hamid, it was awful. It was partly rampant nationalism, and partly a Sunni/Shia fight. There were many fundamentalist aspects to it, many young men were thrown into it as cannon fodder, and in the end it solved nothing other than to leave a million people dead." She shook her head. "The US was quietly backing Saddam Hussein when he was fighting Iran, but when he invaded Kuwait they realized maybe they were backing the wrong person. It's all so ridiculous. Iranians and Americans are much more alike than our governments would want us to believe—we really should be allies instead of mortal enemies. Instead, the US now supports Saudi Arabia like they are the good guys in the region, and the fact is that there is not a more repressive country in the world, especially when it comes to women. Sometimes the stupidity of American foreign policy boggles the mind."

Shane sipped his beer. "Well, we are not always right, but I still wouldn't live anywhere else. Not being a student of the situation but as a casual observer, things are pretty messed up over there. It is a very scary thing, and it all seems to be falling apart. It's hard to fight against someone who is not afraid to die."

CHAPTER THIRTY-EIGHT

Savanna and Sasha were becoming bored with the subject, and Savanna said to Sasha, "I don't know why you're so shy about it. Why does it matter if other people hear us speak Fuqua?"

"Look," said Sasha, "I just like being private, it's not any else's business."

"Why can't it be other people's business?" Savanna shot back. "What is the big deal?"

"Will you shut up, already? I don't want to talk about it!"

"We have to start talking more about things! This big secret bullshit that we've been avoiding for years has got to stop."

"Shut up!" Sasha screamed.

Shane had lost the train of the conversation, not sure if they were still talking about Fuqua. He interjected, "Is there something I'm missing here?"

The two girls just kept their heads down, picking at their food, when Savanna said, "Look, there was an incident when we were freshmen in high school when we were here in Seattle for a semester. We had to leave, end of story."

"What the fuck, Savanna! How can you do this?" screamed Sasha.

"Look, I've stayed a virgin all this time because of you," Savanna shot back. "I have paid my dues over this. It is time for you to move on, and all of us to move on."

Sasha rose to her feet, her face distorted with anger. Before she could do anything, Emma said, "OK, both of you, calm down! Sasha, sit down!"

Sasha sat back down and started crying. Savanna started crying as well, then sheepishly muttered, "I'm sorry."

Shane had no idea what was going on.

Emma turned to him. "Sasha had some intestinal blockage surgery and a tear in her colon when she was a freshman in high school that she was embarrassed about. Once she was better, we headed off to Africa and—"

"It wasn't an intestinal blockage, mother," Sasha interrupted. "It wasn't a tear in my colon. I was raped."

Emma stared at her, stunned. "W-What??" She collapsed back into her chair. Shane was wide-eyed, digesting what he had just heard, not sure if he should leave or stay.

Methodically, in a low steady voice, Sasha directed her conversation to Shane. "We were here for a semester during our freshman year, before we left for Africa. We were at the high school just down the road from here. We didn't know what to expect, we just wanted to get through it. We didn't know anyone. We had just returned from Istanbul where everything was perfect and everyone was wonderful, then we come back to this school where no one understood us or even wanted to be around us. We were the only ones that even looked Middle Eastern, and everyone kind of assumed we were going to bomb the school or something, especially when the word got out that we were Iranian. Everyone was awful to us."

Emma looked like she was going to throw up. Shane was starting to wonder what he had fallen into, and he knew there would be no happy ending.

Sasha continued, her head down but her voice steady. "I asked to go to the bathroom during history, and went down the hall by myself. I had only been in the stall for a few seconds when I heard the door open. Someone with heavy boots was coming toward my stall. I heard a male voice telling me to open the door, I assumed it was a teacher or something, I was confused. I pulled my pants up and opened the stall. As soon as I did he pushed himself into the stall, closed the door behind him, put a knife to my throat and told me if I made any noise he would not hesitate to kill me. I was frozen in fear, I could not move. He spun me around and pulled my pants down and pushed me forward. He forced himself inside me, and stuck something in my ass as he was in me. He had an orgasm in seconds, then pulled out. Then he leaned over, put the knife back in front of my face and grabbed my hair, holding me, and whispered in my ear, 'If anyone ever finds out about this you little Arab cunt, I will kill that bitch sister of yours with this knife and make you watch.' He asked me if I understood and I nodded yes, and he left."

Shane sat there with his mouth agape, shocked at what he had just heard. Everyone was silent. Sasha had still not lifted her gaze. Tears were streaming down the faces of Savanna and Emma.

Finally Emma said, her voice shaking, "Why... why didn't you tell me?"

Sasha lifted her head and looked directly at Emma, and calmly and deliberately said, "Because, mother, you would have found the sharpest knife you had, tracked him down and killed him, just like you did to save us from that asshole in Iran, only this time you would have gone to jail, and we would have been without a mother for the rest our lives."

After a few moments of silence Shane said, "He could still be prosecuted. There is at least a seven-year window on that kind of stuff."

Again, silence. Emma stood and went to Sasha, hugging her from behind without saying anything as she sat in her chair.

Savanna finally broke the silence, directing her conversation to Shane. "Look, it is more complicated than you know. In our culture, on the Iranian side, where much of our family lives in Iran, rape is a disgrace; not to mention the fact that you have lost your virginity. In this country you become the slut who likes to fuck. It is impossible for men to truly understand the consequences of being raped. We could not predict how people would react. It was best to just say nothing, so Sasha and I made a pact that it would be just between us and we did our best to hide it from our mother because we were afraid that we would lose her. Up until now, this has been a sisters' secret, just the two of us, and that is the way we have handled it. Maybe we should have said something sooner, but now is as good a time as any. We are both older now and I think we all need to move on, and I don't think keeping it secret is the best thing anymore."

Sasha then said in a melancholy voice as Emma continued to hug her, "I agree. I didn't realize how much I needed to say that until now. That son of a bitch raped me and took what should have been the best years of my life, and I have been ashamed the whole time, and we have had to hide it like it was my fault." She turned and looked at Emma as Emma stroked her face. "I'm sorry, Mother, that I didn't tell you, but even as I am saying it now I am glad that you didn't know."

"Oh sweetie, I am so sorry I wasn't there for you. I should have somehow seen this. Perhaps I did and refused to believe it. I am so ashamed."

"That is exactly why we didn't say anything mother, everyone would have been ashamed," Savanna said.

"No, I'm not ashamed of what happened to Sasha, I'm ashamed that I was too blind to see what had happened to my own daughter, and ashamed that I was not able to defend her," as she stroked Sasha's hair.

Savanna then said, "Well, l think we did the right thing then, and I still do. I think we should still keep this a secret from the rest of the family. I hope that we can all maybe visit Iran someday and have a relationship with our relatives without it being weird."

Sasha was shaking her head slowly. She said softly, "The way people react to rape in this country and in Iran is absurd, and the older I become the more absurd it seems. Why must women be subjected to this? It wasn't my fault."

Emma sighed. "I don't have a good answer, sweetie. I'm just so sorry this has happened, but it has somehow made both of you wiser than your years. I am so proud of both of you." Emma reached out and took their hands.

"OK," Shane said. "I'm starting to understand the reasons for the secrecy, but it still disturbs me that this asshole is out there without any punishment."

Emma responded "Oh crap, it happens all the time. God will punish the man. At some point, he will pay for his actions."

"That's great," said Shane. "But I prefer retribution and punishment in this lifetime. He has done great damage to your family, and it is not right."

Emma looked directly at him. "We are not going to go public with this, especially now, and I think I can speak for all of us when I ask that you respect our privacy on this matter."

Shane looked at her, took a deep breath, and said, "Yes, I will respect this secret. And Sasha," he turned to look directly at her. "I want to apologize for what has happened to you, as a man... as an American man... it is not fair, and it was in no way your fault. There are men out there in the world you can trust."

Sasha smiled at Shane, her face relaxing.

They all sat there for a while, finishing their food in silence. Everyone needed a break from talking. There seemed to be a new closeness among the four of them; the devastating conversation had built what seemed like years of familiarity. The rape was deeply disturbing, but Shane felt strangely protective of this family he hardly knew, and he liked it very much.

When he looked at Emma, another feeling rose that he just couldn't figure out. It wasn't love, exactly, but more a feeling that there was more to their encounter than he knew.

CHAPTER THIRTY-NINE

"Let's all go out tonight," Shane said, after they had cleared away the dinner dishes and relaxed for a few hours. "You ladies can get all dolled up, we can drive down to Ballard's Cues and Brews, play some pool and dance a little. There is a fun band playing, maybe we can change the mood here. I know I could use a drink."

"Sounds like a classy place," said Emma jokingly.

"Well it's nearby, clean, and has a nice dance floor, and I've seen this band before. They're good."

They all smiled at the thought of getting dressed up and listening to some music. The women had been living in relative isolation for some time now, and there just weren't a lot of things to do up on the island.

"Well, we could, just for a little while," Emma said. "It's been a pretty exhausting couple of days. I'll need to change the dressings on your hands. Are you sure you're up to it?"

"My legs are fine, hands feel pretty good, hernia not bursting out of my gut or anything." He smiled. "I can handle it, yes."

"Girls?" asked Emma.

"Yes!" they both said simultaneously. Getting out for some live music sounded fabulous, and both were feeling much better after the afternoon cry-fest.

"OK, then," said Shane. "Bus leaves in an hour."

"It leaves when we're ready," said Emma.

"Yes, of course," said Shane in an exaggeratedly submissive voice.

Smiling, Emma headed to her room, as did the girls. Shane was ready five minutes later, then proceeded to sit on the couch and wait for his dates for the next hour and a half. When they were all ready, he couldn't believe what was in front of him. The women were an exotic blend of cultures; Emma's beautiful head scarf contrasting and complimenting her body-hugging black dress, the girls in stunningly beautiful and colorful dresses they had picked up in Istanbul.

"So you just happened to have these outfits in your weekend bags?" Shane asked somewhat sarcastically, staring at the women with a smile.

"It's always good to be prepared for anything," said Emma chuckling. "OK, enough ogling, lets just head down there and have a little fun, for once."

"You do realize this is a beer pub with a dance floor, correct?"

"Yes Shane, we realize that. Can't three girls get dressed up for some dancing now and then without being judged?" Emma shook her hips in a disco fashion and pointed to the sky, much to the girls' delight.

"OK, then! Head-em up and move-em out, we're burning daylight." It was one of Shane's favorite expressions, but the looks on the three women's faces told him not to use it again.

The parking lot and exterior of the pub was less than impressive, evoking an "ewww," from Savanna.

Shane smiled. "Well, it's not much aesthetically, but it's kind of a fun place. Plus they have a dinner area so you youngsters are allowed in."

"Pfff, youngsters," scoffed Sasha.

It was nine p.m. and dark by the time they arrived, and when they walked in, every eye in the room turned to look at them. Actually, all eyes were ignoring the bandaged man and fixated on the women. Their dresses and high heels made them look like they were headed to a much nicer place. Even the band was thrown off a bit during their rendition of Robert Palmer's "Irresistible," which was the perfect song for their arrival.

They were able to get a nice booth away from the stage. It was still early and the pub was only about half full, but a steady stream of new faces began showing up. The girls were smiling and looking lovely, and Emma seemed to have a continuous smirk on her face that was slowly evolving into a smile.

Shane was patting himself on the back for thinking of taking them out, as the band ended its song. Emma smiled and turned to Shane. "Can we get something to drink, please?"

Shane and Emma soon had vodka tonics in front of them. The girls settled on sodas, both looking at the stage and moving in rhythm with the energetic band.

There were probably a half dozen people on the dance floor when Shane turned to Emma. "Shall we?"

Emma just laughed and said "sure," dragging and encouraging the girls along with her. The four of them were able to ignore everyone else in the room as they filled the dance floor with energy. Shane with his bandaged hands was trying to keep beat to the music and doing his best bad dancer routine. He took it easy because of his hernia, but the girls must have been secretly dancing together for years in their room or something, he thought. They were moving together like movie stars on the dance floor.

Between Emma and the two young exotic beauties, he was the envy of every man in the room.

The girls were completely ignoring everything, especially their mom and Shane, and dancing like they didn't have a care in the world. After a few songs, they all laughed and danced their way back to the booth, as the band decided to take a break, thanking everyone for the great energy out on the dance floor.

They had settled back into the booth when three men walked by close to the table and exited to the parking lot. Shane was still catching his breath, blinking to clear the sweat from his eyes and wiping his brow. He took a drink of his vodka tonic and looked at Emma, then the girls.

Sasha had her head buried, Savanna was stroking her hand.

"Who was that?" asked Shane.

Sasha still had her head down, just shaking her head. Savanna then sadly said, "That was Mikey. He's the one that raped Sasha. He must still live around here."

"We are just going to sit here and stay calm" said Emma, still catching her breath.

"Jesus," said Shane, "now what?"

"Now nothing," said Emma, "what are we supposed to do?"

"I just want to go home," said Sasha.

"OK," said Emma. "We'll go home, sweetie. We can talk about this later if you want."

"I don't want to talk about it, I just want to go home," Sasha said.

Shane stood, walked up to the hostess and paid the tab.

As they walked out the door and headed to the car, they could see that the three men were hanging out at the far end of the parking lot, smoking. Shane opened the doors for the dressed-up women, then walked around to his side. The three men were walking toward the car.

As Shane reached for his door handle, he looked at them, and one of them yelled, "What the fuck are you looking at, old man?"

He didn't respond, just continued to get into the car. But before he could lock the doors, one of the men rushed to Shane's door and started to pull him out.

"What the fuck are you doing?" yelled Shane, putting up more resistance than expected. A second man joined in, pulling and yanking Shane from the car. The third man said, "We're gonna teach you a lesson, you Arab-loving motherfucker."

They pulled and dragged him away from the car, kicking and punching the now fully resisting man, ignoring the women. Emma was in a panic, trying to think through the situation, losing sight of Shane as he was dragged to the front of the car.

"No no no no," Sasha cried, her voice growing louder and louder.

Emma said firmly, "Sasha, calm down, we are not going to do anything. Calm down!"

Sasha then screamed "Nooo!" She opened her door and sprinted at the melee, now thirty feet from the car, kicking her heels off on the way.

"Shit!" said Emma. She got out of the car, followed closely by Savanna. People in the bar had been alerted to the ruckus in the parking lot, and were pouring out of the bar. Mikey was directly on top of Shane, wildly punching at the struggling man, while the other two men were on either side, trying to hold him down.

Mikey didn't see Sasha coming. He was very drunk and completely focused on beating the crap out of the Arab-loving man beneath him. With a flying leap over the final five feet, and at full speed, she clamped onto his back, wrapped her legs around him, and viciously bit into his ear. He stood and let out a scream, which distracted his two friends from the man on the ground. By the time they saw the crazed girl on Mikey's back, the two other women had reached the scene, heels in hand. Emma and Savanna each took aim at the other two men, viciously whipping the men with their heels. The men screamed and swatted wildly at the unexpected attack.

Shane jumped to his feet, and as one of the men spun away from the heel attack, he turned directly into a full-force and perfectly aimed head butt from Shane. The man's nose shattered. He was instantly bleeding everywhere and stumbled aimlessly away from the fray, blood spurting from his face, much to the horror of the growing audience.

The other man turned and stumbled into the killing zone, flailing with his arms to counter the vicious attacks from the whipping heels. He turned into Shane and in the next moment Shane kicked as hard as he could into the man's crotch. The man collapsed, both women still beating him with their heels as he fell to the fetal position on the ground.

Sasha was still clamped onto Mikey's ear. He was spinning wildly, trying to get her off of his back, when Shane took a hop and skip and in the next motion, with his bandaged right hand, hit Mikey square in the jaw. Mikey spun into the straight right punch... he dropped to his knees with a cross-eyed look, then fell face first, Sasha riding him all the way down, still locked onto his ear.

Shane glanced down to see that his arm had been shattered at the forearm, the bone partially sticking out of the skin. His hernia throbbed. Ignoring his injuries, he turned to the women still beating the now-defenseless man in the fetal position. "Emma!" he yelled, breaking her out of her trance. "Get in the car!"

Emma and Savanna both scrambled upright and raced for the car, then Emma wheeled back to snatch up her purse lying in the sidewalk. Shane reached down and pulled Sasha off Mikey with his good arm. She was kicking and wailing and wouldn't let go, but he was finally able to pry her off. Blood spurted from Mikey's head.

Shane carried Sasha over to the car with his one working arm. She was screaming as if she'd completely lost her mind, her face and dress covered in blood.

People continued to spill out of the bar. There were screams of "Oh my God!" and "Call 911!"

Shane reached the car carrying a still-struggling Sasha. He yelled, "Everyone get in the fucking car!" They all scrambled in,

Savanna taking hold of Sasha, trying to calm her down. Emma started the car.

"I'll be right back," said Shane.

Emma said, "Shane, get back here!" But he didn't listen.

He pulled out a locking knife from his pocket with his left hand, his right hand hanging by his side, dripping blood.

Mikey was moving to his knees, then he was on all fours, with a gun in his hand. Shane saw the gun and with a swift kick sent it flying and spinning across the parking lot. As it hit the rock wall, a gunshot went off and ricocheted through the parking lot.

The crowd watching screamed and scattered, a dozen people ducking and scrambling for safety, the parking lot instantly devoid of people other than the brutal fight's participants.

Shane kicked Mikey hard on his side and flipped him onto his back as he squatted over the delirious man, opened the locking knife with his teeth. He put the knife right in front of Mikey's face.

Mikey was now lying on his back, defenseless under a possessed man with a knife, barely conscious, ear apparently missing. The other men were completely disabled, one bleeding profusely from his nose, staggering around the parking lot, begging for anyone to help. The other man still lying in the fetal position on the ground, groaning in agony.

Shane leaned down, and in a sinister voice said, "This is my dad's deer knife, you sick fuck. Do you know what this is used for?"

Mikey gave a weak nod.

"That's good. Because if you ever disrespect, or even come close to, one of those women again, I swear on the grave of my dead father that I will track you down if it is the last thing I do and gut you with this knife, you piece of shit. Do you believe me when I tell you that?"

Mikey gave Shane another terrified nod.

"Good, then we have an understanding."

Shane closed the knife and put it back in his pocket as he stood and calmly walked back to the car. When he got in, the women were all staring at him, stunned.

Shane turned to Emma. "Go." She slammed on the accelerator. Unfortunately, in her confusion and panic the car was in reverse, and she crashed into the building, causing a sign to fall from the side wall. Dust flew everywhere and the girls were screaming in the back. Shane turned to Emma again. She looked at him with a terrified expression, and he pointed forward with his one working arm. "That way."

She put the car in drive and tore out of the parking lot. Within half a block, ambulances and police cars were screaming to the scene. None of them in the car said anything for a moment, then Emma caught sight of Shane's arm.

"Oh my God." Emma pulled over on a side street and ran around to his side of the car. She tore off her headscarf and made a quick tourniquet to stop the bleeding. "I can't fix this," she said. "We have to go to the emergency room."

Shane just shrugged and said "You're the doc." Emma got back into the driver's seat and they headed off to the hospital.

CHAPTER FORTY

The detective walked in and surveyed the hospital room. He saw three well-dressed, disheveled women, one covered in blood, and a man with a full cast on his elevated right arm, bandages on his hands, contusions all over his face, a swollen eye, and a huge lump on his forehead.

"Ok then," said the detective, nodding his head, slowly looking at each person. "I'm Detective Lou Olsen from the Seattle Police Department," he said, flashing his credentials. "I don't usually get midnight wakeup calls for bar fights, but this one was the exception. I had a twenty-year police officer first on the scene and he said he'd never seen anything like it. Now I've got three thugs in the hospital, one in critical condition and missing an ear, one with a ruptured testicle that will need to be removed, and the third with a broken nose and crushed eye socket. Can somebody explain exactly what the hell happened?"

They all looked at each other. Shane had just opened his mouth to speak when another man stepped into the room. "Detective, a word please?"

The detective raised his eyebrows, gave a frustrated grunt and walked out into the hallway with the man. Shane looked at Emma and she rolled her eyes in a manner that said she knew what it was about.

"Never a dull moment," was all Shane could come up with.

Out in the hallway, the two men talked. "I'm Anthony Bodela," the newcomer said. "I'm am with the US Secret Service from here in the Seattle office. We have something of a delicate situation here." He showed the detective his credentials and they shook hands.

A clearly irritated Detective Olson said, "And the reason you are interrupting a crime investigation is?"

"Well," said Bodela, being as respectful as possible. "The older woman in that room is under the watch of the Secret Service, to protect her from an assassination attempt by a foreign government. She is not directly protected, but we try our best to help her. It's a long story, but it's important that we do our best to protect her identity."

"So, are you're suggesting that she is immune to our laws?" asked the detective, still obviously miffed at the intrusion.

"No, no," said Bodela, "We just need you to go through your procedure as quietly as possible. No pictures, no news media, it needs to be kept out of the spotlight. The full resources of our office will be available to you. We want to know the truth of what happened as well, but without dipping into the national security vault if we can avoid it. We will need to work together on this one as much as possible."

Detective Olson thought for a moment. "OK, come on in. I'm not sure what the right protocol is here, but I appreciate you being straight with me."

"Thanks," said Bodela. They both went back into the room.

"OK, this is a Mr. Bodela, he will be joining us in the conversation," the detective said without explaining. "Now where was I? Oh yeah, three thugs were beat up in the parking lot at Ballard Cues and Brews. Anybody want to start?"

After a moment's silence, Shane said, "No disrespect, Detective, but I'm thinking we might need to speak to an attorney first."

"Well," said the detective. "If we are claiming self-defense, which I have to assume is the case, you shouldn't need an attorney."

Shane thought for a moment. "Well basically, they thought that I looked at them wrong as we were getting into our car, so they dragged me out and started pounding me. The women came to my defense and we ended up winning the war."

The detective chuckled. "It was a war," he agreed. "I mean one guy in the ICU, another needing surgery, and then there is the ear—we still haven't found that thing." There was a moment of silence. "Look," he said. "Your description is basically what we are getting from witnesses, but there was a gunshot and a knife that need some explaining."

Shane nodded. "Well, I kicked the gun out of his hand. The hammer must have hit the wall and it went off. No one pulled the trigger. And as for the knife, I felt a very clear and concise message needed to be sent that they needed to stay away from these women, once and for all."

The detective looked at Shane, sizing him up, then looked again around the room. "OK," he said, taking his time. "That's all fine, but what I don't understand... " he slowly looked at each person in turn. "What I don't quite get, is the intensity of the fight. Did they know you ladies? Was there another incident?"

The room was silent. "Look, these guys all have violent records," the detective added. "If something happened, I would love to know about it so I can put them away."

"Well, officer, there was—" Shane started.

"No!" Sasha yelled. She was looking directly at the startled detective. She stood up and walked toward him, then in a strong, firm voice said "It is an eye for an eye, and a tooth for a tooth! It is over!" She pointed at his chest.

Sasha stood there in front of the detective, with the blood all over her dress and small cuts and scrapes everywhere, not flinching from the detective's eyes. The anger and determination in her face was something her mother had never seen before, prior to her clamping on Mikey's ear a few hours earlier.

The detective nodded as they stared at each other, then gently waved Sasha back to her seat. He thought for a moment, rubbing his chin and again scanning the room. "OK," he said, "my initial reaction is that this was self-defense, pure and simple, and I will not be recommending charges. But I can make no promises. If our friend Mikey dies, it will get more complicated. I think the chances of the DA bringing charges are slim with these guys involved; he's had to deal with them too many times on the other end of the bloodshed. It might end up being one of those just-desserts type things."

He turned to the agent standing behind him. "Mr. Bodela here tells me that we need to keep this as quiet as possible and I will do my best, but I give no guarantees. We can't control everything." He passed out a card to everyone. "Last thing, if you ever hear even a peep from these guys again, here is my card with my cell number on it, call me directly." He shook everyone's hand. "That's it for now, but I will likely need to talk to you some more, so I will be in touch."

"Thank you officer," Emma said. When he had left, she turned to Bodela. "Well, Anthony, sorry to bring you into this, but it really wasn't our fault."

"Yeah," said Bodela. "I'm just glad you're OK. What a nightmare. I think we can keep your name out of the paper, but if someone had a camera, your face might show up. We will just have to play it by ear, no pun intended." No one laughed. He shook her hand and said his goodbyes.

After he left the room Shane said to Emma, "Let me guess: story for another time?"

Emma looked at him and smirked. "Yes, I will tell you that part as well, but I think now rest would be good."

Shane turned his attention to Sasha. "What the hell did you do with his ear?" Everyone looked at her.

She gave them a bewildered look. "I don't know what happened to the thing. I didn't swallow it, for fuck's sake!"

"Ewww," Savanna said, as Shane and Emma both recoiled a bit and dropped the subject.

Shane looked at Emma. "Why don't you and the girls go home, get cleaned up, and get some sleep. Then we can catch up later. I want to get out of here as soon as possible, but I really don't feel like moving at the moment."

"OK," said Emma. "Girls, let's head out." The girls got up, and started to walk out with their mom. Sasha turned around went back to Shane and gave him a gentle kiss on the cheek, followed by Savanna, who kissed his other cheek. Emma thought for a moment, then went over and gave him a kiss on the forehead, carefully avoiding the lump. Then they all left the room. Shane was sound asleep before the door was fully shut.

CHAPTER FORTY-ONE

Shane didn't know how long he had been sleeping when the nurse came in, leaving the morning paper and a pot of coffee in a plastic carafe. He saw that it was nine a.m.; the few hours of sleep had left him feeling great. He groaned as he shifted in his bed, his hernia protesting the movement. He was able to pour himself a coffee with bandaged hands. He ignored the urge to brush his teeth and sipped on what was obviously canned coffee, which for some reason still tasted great. He grabbed the paper and flopped it onto his lap. Before he even had his glasses on, he said, "Oh shit."

On the front page of the paper was a picture of the prior night's activities, somewhat blurred and dark, but Emma and the girls were clearly visible, and Shane was shown walking toward Mikey. The caption read 'Wild melee in Ballard.'

As he was reading it, the nurse walked in again with a menu and a smile. "Well hello, Mr. Melee."

Shane gave her an exasperated look. "Yeah, I guess it was inevitable. Cameras are everywhere these days."

Shane was able to get some breakfast and cleaned himself up a bit before Emma arrived, an hour later. His arm was still throbbing, but he was hoping they would release him if he didn't complain too much. She walked into the room, looking surprisingly refreshed after a crazy night and not much sleep. In fact, she looked beautiful.

He was staring at her with a loving look on his face. "What?! she said, snapping him out of his trance.

"Just thinking you look awfully good, considering what we went through last night."

"Bah," said Emma. "It's a Persian thing. Men don't let us sleep much over there."

Shane laughed, hoping it was a joke, and was relieved when she laughed back.

"Can we go home now?" he said in his most pathetic voice.

"I don't know," snapped Emma. "What did the doctor say?"

"I haven't seen one until now," Shane shot back.

"Can't you release me?"

Emma laughed. "No, you need a doctor here to release you, my dear."

Just then the doctor walked in. "Well, well, you two must be the brawlers of Ballard?" He looked down at the newspaper on Shane's table.

"Oh yeah," said Shane to Emma. "I forgot to show that to you."

Emma looked at it and gasped. "Oh my God!"

"Well it's kind of fuzzy and you can't really see your face," Shane said, trying to keep her from panicking.

"Well, I just hope my bosses don't see it or put two and two together, or I'm going to have a lot of explaining to do." She picked up the paper and skimmed the article. "At least our names aren't in here."

The doctor cut in. "How is the arm feeling? And tell me about all the burns. When did that happen?"

"It's a long story," said Shane. "Let's just say the last forty-eight hours have been eventful."

The doctor examined the bandages and the cast, satisfying himself that everything looked alright. "You're going to need some healing time. We don't need to keep you here, but you need to keep that arm elevated at all times, and use a sling for at least a couple of weeks. Your head looks clear; the brain scan didn't show any problems. We had a good surgeon on call last night, he was confident the arm set well. You might need a second surgery, but for now give it some rest. No more scuffles. We will need to take a look at it again in a week or so."

"No more scuffles, promise," said Shane.

He was greatly looking forward to sitting on the couch, turning on the tube for some sports, and cracking a beer, or better yet having one cracked for him. It was all he could think about on the way home.

"You're on some pretty heavy pain killers, so no alcohol," said Emma, reading his thoughts. "And how's the hernia doing?"

Shane moaned, "Oh, for Christ's sake. Can we hold off on the painkillers so I can have a beer? I think I've earned one. Hernia seems OK, and please don't have the girls examine me again."

Emma laughed loudly. OK, no hernia examine, and maybe one beer, but that's it, and no driving."

"Yeah, like I was planning on driving anytime in the next week," Shane deadpanned. Smirk.

Emma smiled over at him. She enjoyed his sense of humor. Simple-minded American doofus, yes, but still cute and funny, and capable of moments of extreme bravery. She was glad he was on their side.

CHAPTER FORTY-TWO

"What should we do for him?" said Savanna as they sat on their bed in the guest house. Sasha just gave her a questioning look. Usually she knew exactly what Savanna meant, but not this time.

"Well, I'm just saying," Savanna continued, "he was very brave last night, and I think he deserves some special treatment."

"I don't think mom would approve."

"Jesus, do you hear yourself talk sometimes? The guy got the crap kicked out of him for us last night, I think we could do something to show our appreciation." Savanna wiggled her eyebrows.

"OK fine," said Sasha, suspiciously smiling. "What do you suggest?"

"Hmm," said Savanna in her most devious voice. "What about a Puuuursian belly dance? It would be fun."

"I don't know," said Sasha.

"Trust me," Savanna said. "It will be good for you."

Sasha sighed heavily. "OK, fine." They set about planning the night's surprise.

The afternoon was thankfully quite uneventful, with the girls secretly preparing for Shane's present later that evening. Emma ignored what they were up to and mostly doted over Shane. He was lying on the couch, working on his second beer, when she decided she had to say something.

"Your choice, beer or pain pills. I hate to sound like a doctor but I can't be party to your little party anymore."

"OK then, I'll go with a third beer, fuck the pain pills."

If nothing else, the admission was a reality check for Emma. Every time she started to think he was a guy she could be with, he managed to jolt her back into reality. But she still thought he was cute and funny and brave and... stop! She had to stop going there. Nothing was going to happen, she quietly reminded herself.

Although it had been sixteen years since she had been with a man, she figured that even Hamid would forgive her at this point. Despite that, her mind would often go to Hamid whenever she considered being with another man. It was impossible and frustrating, because there could never be another love like him, she knew that. Anything else would be temporary.

But if she used a temporary marriage contract, at least it would be somewhat legitimate in her faith. Even though she didn't consider herself a practicing Muslim, she did still appreciate the security and morality and guidance that her faith provided, and at times wished her daughters would be more interested. She could see them falling more and more into a western mindset, and found it disturbing.

Emma worked her way out to the back deck to have some alone time to think. Shane seemed to be perfectly happy working on his beer and channel surfing for sports.

As she sat with her coffee, looking at Shane's garden, her mind went to worrying about the girls, who were now so far from Islam that they were even growing uncomfortable with their own mother's modesty. Were they falling into a life of sexual promiscuity and all of the ramifications that went along with it? Would they find out too late that the life that they were in was not the only answer? As Emma pondered, her heart ached.

Raising the girls without a father was more difficult than she had ever dreamed. She tried her best to keep them living with a moral compass, but could see that she was failing. The brawl at the bar was satisfying in that she knew they were not afraid of standing up for themselves. Come to think of it, she had not seen that type of behavior in Sasha for years. It was good that she bit that rapist's ear off. Sasha's comment about an eye for an eye and tooth for a tooth was a very Islamic thing, but Emma had never taught her that. It must have come from somewhere deep inside.

If the girls were to survive in the world, especially in this western world that she had brought them up in, they would have to be tough and strong. They had certainly shown fearlessness the night before. But what about temptation, decency, morality? Would they be able to live a respectable life in a country and society that fostered sexuality and depraved behavior?

Freedom comes at a high cost at times, she thought. If there were only a way to blend the two worlds, or at least to have respect and mutual understanding, it would be best, but it seemed to be an impossible dream.

Shane brought her out of her thoughts when he poked his head out the back door. "Any plans for dinner?"

Emma looked at him, with beer in hand and a goofy look on his face. "Steak and potatoes?"

"Oh yeah, that would be awesome," Shane said, the beers in him speaking before his brain. "Wait. Joking, right?"

"Yes, that would be a joke. I can make a lovely Persian meal later that I'm sure you will find just as satisfying."

"I'm in, sounds great," Shane said, trying to recover.

The girls, meanwhile, had returned from a local shopping venture. "So where have you two been?" asked Emma as she walked inside with Shane.

"Nowhere, just picking up a few things," Savanna said in her usual mischievous voice.

Emma didn't think anything of it. "Don't forget," she said, "you have a gynecologist appointment tomorrow after we drop you off at school, it's at the clinic on Fifteenth Street."

Savanna had forgotten. "I hate those. Who is the doctor, do you know her?"

"It's not a her, it's a him. Sheila is on vacation, so her associate is covering her clients while she is gone."

"Is he at least a Muslim, for fuck's sake?" Savanna demanded.

Emma just laughed at that. "What difference does it make?"

"Well, at least I could do a sighe contract with a Muslim for an hour or something, so he could look at my vagina!"

Shane was once again a fly on the wall in their conversation, and he was finding it quite entertaining.

"You will be fine," said Emma. "And no, you can't get a sighe contract for an hour to see a gynecologist, that's not what it is for."

"Argggh," Savanna moaned. She stomped into the bedroom with Sasha and their purchases, Sasha trying to suppress her laughter.

With the girls' door closed, Shane let out a suppressed laugh. "Savanna has quite the sense of humor. At least I think that was supposed to be humorous."

Emma chuckled. "I'm never quite sure with that one, but I think she was half-serious. I'm just glad she is becoming curious about some of the nicer Islamic customs. A sighe contract is one that would be useful in this country, but I'm afraid most western men would use it as an excuse for adultery, which is not its intent."

"OK, I'll bite," Shane said. "What exactly is a sighe contract?"

Emma poured herself a small glass of wine without offering Shane one, and explained the sighe. "But virgins cannot do a sexual sighe contract," she finished. "Islam is very clear on that. Only the father can release her virginity to her permanent husband."

Shane wasn't sure whether to laugh, because he wasn't sure if she was joking. Since she hadn't laughed, he supposed she must be serious.

Emma went on. "You have the terms spelled out in the contract, including the end date, whether it will be sexual, what the dowry is, and so on. It gives a woman the chance to back out if it doesn't work out. Once in a permanent marriage, the woman cannot get a divorce without the man's permission."

"Ouch," said Shane. "That seems pretty unfair."

"The woman has the option to not go through with a permanent marriage after the term of the sighe ends, however. It just means that women need to be very careful not to get into a permanent marriage that they are not sure about, and overall it works pretty well. Most western scholars think it is Islam's way of legalizing prostitution, as often there is a dowry included in the contract, but that is usually not the case. Providing a dowry is more to show that the man has the means to support the woman in the future."

"Well, it is so far from the norm here that it is hard to understand," said Shane.

Emma just nodded. She appreciated his honesty.

They sat together for a few minutes, then Emma said, "I need to go down to the store and get a few things for dinner. Do you have everything you need?"

"Well, one last beer would be good. I promise to nurse it like a baby," Shane begged.

She frowned, but went to the fridge, pulled out another beer, cracked it open and handed it to him, then grabbed her purse and said, "I'll be back in a bit."

"Yum," said Shane, "I love it already," intentionally sounding like a lush. She just smiled and headed out. While she was gone he was able to track down the last inning of the Mariners game, much to his delight, and settled in to watch a one-run pitcher's duel. Not his favorite type of game—he preferred lots of runs and hits—but any baseball was good baseball, was his philosophy. Soon the game was over, and he sat there for a few minutes channel surfing, trying to appreciate the last few sips of beer. Then he heard the girls turn on what sounded like Arabic (Persian, he silently reminded himself) music.

The door to their bedroom opened and the girls slowly started out with the boom box leading the way, gyrating their way out the door, setting the music on the table, and dancing their way to Shane in extremely skimpy Persian outfits, like tiny bikinis with tassels and little ropes. Each wore an elaborate headdress. The music was something Shane had not heard before, but he assumed it was belly dancing music, because that was what they appeared to be doing. They worked their way closer to Shane as he sat there frozen, afraid to move.

Savanna closed in ever so close to Shane's face with her breasts barely covered, got down close to his ear, and in beat with the music said "We are not Iranian, we are Purrrrrrsian... " drawing out the Persian to sound like a purring cat with a Middle Eastern accent.

Shane was dumbfounded. The girls were dancing in front of him almost naked. They were eighteen and, he guessed, legal, and God they were sexy. But why was this happening? Emma would be home soon and he'd probably be in trouble. And holy shit, it was hot.

They were moving in sync with each other like they had been practicing for years for this moment. They danced around the room in paced unison, chanting to the music and snapping their fingers together. They would take turns sensually running a silk scarf over his head and down his lap. Shane sat there, afraid to move.

The music was so loud that no one heard the car pull into the carport.

Emma could not begin to understand the reason for the music she was hearing. When she opened the door, the vision that she saw would be burned forever into her memory. Both girls had their butts inches from Shane's face, impressively shaking them belly dance style. Shane was sitting there with a perplexed look on his face.

This time it was Emma's turn to scream. She went over, turned off the music, and pointed to the bedroom. "Out, out, out!"

"Oh Mother, relax," Savanna said. "We just wanted to do something special for him."

Furious, she gave one last bellow. "Out!" As the now-distressed girls went into the bedroom and shut the door.

Shane was sitting on the couch with a truly terrified look on his face. "I don't know how to explain that, I really had nothing to do with it," he blurted, like a little boy about to be punished.

Emma sat on the side couch and just stared ahead, rocking back and forth, still absorbing what she had just seen. Shane went on "I don't think they meant anything weird, I just think they were—"

Emma cut him off. "Can you leave for a bit, so I can have a word with my daughters?"

"Yes, yes, of course. I'll take a walk, I could use some air. Back in an hour."

"Thank you," said Emma. Shane got up, grabbed his wallet and keys and headed out, greatly relieved to be out of the firing line.

Emma took a deep breath, thought for a few moments, then stood and walked over to the girls' room. "Girls, please come out here when you have some clothes on, we need to have a talk."

Savanna and Sasha were sitting on the bed, looking at each other. Savanna softly said, "fuck." Sasha replied, "Fuck is right; she sounds pretty pissed."

They both dressed, and hesitantly opened the door to see their mother sitting on the couch waiting for them. They approached and sat across from her. They had never really seen her this mad at them, and had no idea what to expect, but they knew that they needed to be quiet.

Emma turned and looked straight at them. "Have I not been a good mother? Have I not instilled at least some values and morality into your lives? What is it that brought you to the point that you would think this display to Shane would be acceptable? Do you think that flashing your bodies will get you respect and loyalty and love in life?"

The girls hesitated, both looking down. Finally Savanna spoke. "I'm sorry, Mother. This was just a playful thing that I thought would be fun. We didn't think that deeply about it."

Emma let out a big sigh. "That is an understatement. Savanna, Sasha, when your father died, I was forced into a situation that I look back on and almost wish I would have handled it differently. There are many beautiful things about living life in Iran, living an Islamic life, living with morality and decency. There are also many beautiful things about living here; you have so much more freedom and rights as women. But if you take those rights, that freedom, and become visual objects for men, then that is how the world will define you. You will get no respect, and you will have no moral base to live your life. You must be able to find it within yourself, find your own calling, reach down deep and draw from the souls of your ancestors, from your father's soul, and from me, and understand that there is nothing more important to a young woman than her dignity. This is true in Iran, and it is true here."

Emma paused. "I understand that you think of life as a game sometimes, but in order to get respect, you must act accordingly. I cannot be there for you going forward. You are now adults and will be making your own decisions, that is the way it works in this country. I have brought you as far as I can, and this is one of the last times that I am going to be able to help, to try to provide some guidance as a mother. You will need to make your own choices now. It is not like in Iran, where you would have family and relatives around all the time, and a society to help you grow. Here you are free to make your own choices, but you must use that freedom wisely, or it will destroy you. It will turn you into objects of men's desires, and nothing else. Do you understand what I am saying?"

Both girls had tears streaming down their faces. Unable to speak, they just nodded.

"Good," said Emma. "Now if you would help me to prepare a nice meal for Shane, that would be just as much of a reward to him as your little dance. He can be a pretty simple-minded fellow." Both giggled through their tears, and they all stood and headed to the kitchen.

CHAPTER FORTY-THREE

When Shane returned later for dinner, he had no idea what to expect. He even thought that perhaps the car would be gone and he would never see the three women again. The weekend had been so bizarre that anything was possible. When he opened the door he saw the table, spread with a beautiful array of interesting-looking dishes, many of which he did not recognize. He looked toward the kitchen and saw the three women still cooking away. All three were wearing beautiful, loose-fitting head scarves, and all were dressed very modestly, a far cry from what he had seen earlier that day. Whatever Emma had said, something had changed pretty dramatically. But he decided not to ask, and just greeted them with a simple, "Hello, ladies. Looks and smells delicious."

They all smiled and nodded, then Emma explained the meal to him. "We are doing a Nowruz dinner, a Persian celebration of a new year. At least, we are trying our best with the ingredients we could find. The stores here are pretty good for the food itself, but I couldn't find all of the spices. You actually have a decent spice rack up here. I am impressed."

"Well, don't be too impressed," said Shane. "Most of those came from guests coming and going. I've had quite a variety of people coming through and they leave things."

"Have you had some Persians through?" Emma asked.

Shane hesitated, thinking of the best way to not sound ignorant. "Middle Eastern, yes. No belly dancing, though," he said with a smirk.

"Oh, shut up!" said Savanna, shocked by the comment and hoping it wouldn't stir up her mom again.

"Sorry," said Shane, chuckling under his breath. "I did have quite a variety of people, actually. The worst ones were a group of young kids from Canada—I think they were Middle Eastern or Indian or something, but they had this giant eight-legged bong that they were sucking on all night; it vibrated through the floor down into my bedroom. It sounded like a Cheech and Chong movie till four in the morning."

All the women laughed. "That would be a hookah, and you're right, they probably were from the Middle East somewhere," said Emma.

Shane was greatly appreciative that the little erotic dance earlier was apparently forgotten. He regretted bringing it up as a joke, but they seemed to be OK about it. Emma chuckled at his honesty as she continued in the kitchen.

"So, I'd love to hear more about the meal," Shane said.

"The Nowruz." Emma said the name slowly so he would understand. "It is typically held on the first day of spring, symbolizing a new year, or rebirth. It's not the spring now, of course, but we wanted to have it anyway. The items displayed on the table represent the seven guardian angels of the New Year. There is light or sunrise, patience, affluence, love, health, beauty, and medicine. It is more complicated than that, but that is essentially what is happening. In Iran, it typically goes on for thirteen days, and on the thirteenth day there is a big outdoor feast for family and friends. It is a lovely tradition, one that we all enjoy greatly. It is not a religious tradition, but more about symbolism and family and thanking the world for giving new life to a new growing season—starting over, if you will, and being thankful as a community for all that you have been blessed with."

"Huh," said Shane, still trying to remember how to pronounce it. Now rooz? Whatever it was, it was smelling more and more delicious to him. He was wondering if alcohol was included, but decided not to ask. There were bean dishes, some types of dark green vegetables, and those finger-sized things with grape leaves and rice in the middle that he would actually buy now and then, but he was guessing the ones in front of him didn't come from a can.

There were lots of egg dishes, too, and the smell of garlic wafted up from the table. They soon sat down and he waited for instructions on when to start. After a few moments of no one moving, Emma said "As the guest at the table, it is proper for you to start, please help yourself." She smiled at Shane and gestured toward the food.

"OK then, yum," said Shane, and he started to load his plate.

As he filled up his plate he started talking to Emma, "So I walked down and had a chat with the bar owner about your handiwork on his building. He would prefer to keep the whole thing as quiet and under the table as possible, meaning if we throw him a grand in cash he would probably be happy."

"I'll pay for that," said Emma without hesitating. "I would prefer it to be as quiet as possible as well. That picture of us in the paper was enough. I could go to the bank tomorrow and perhaps we could stop by there after dropping the girls off at the university."

"Sounds good," said Shane, and once the women had served themselves he dove in to the most delicious meal he'd ever eaten.

CHAPTER FORTY-FOUR

The next day Sasha and Savanna loaded up the new car and the four of them headed out to the university. They both had stylish scarves on their heads. They had decided jointly to add a little color, but also to go with modesty and a stylish Persian look, and just see what happened.

They drove the Subaru to campus because Emma had taken the Mazda to the body shop and left it there to get the damage repaired. "The car should be fixed in about a week," she said to the girls. "You'll have to just use the bus until then." They arrived at the main parking area and all headed toward the main entrance. Shane plodded alongside with his bruised face, arm in a sling and bandaged hands.

It was impossible for them to not draw attention as they walked through the campus. Pods of families and students were working their way to as-yet-undiscovered buildings, maps in hand, sounding confused. All would be distracted for a moment and look at the three women and beaten-up man walking past. As they neared their building, they all stopped and Emma said, "Well, I think this is it."

The girls had already begun crying, Shane stepped back to give them space.

Emma was hugging her two lovely girls, smiling and stroking their hair. "I love you both more than you possibly know, and you know that I will always be there for you, right?" The girls nodded with tears pouring down their cheeks, both hugging their mother as tightly as they could. "I could not be more proud of you," said Emma.

After hugging their mom, they each went to Shane and put out their hand. Shane smiled like a proud father and reached out with his left hand. "Thank you," they said simply. Shane was grateful to them for making the goodbye so easy.

As the girls started to walk away, three young men approached from the other direction. One pointed at the girls and said "Look, a couple of Arab hotties." The girls froze in their tracks, much to the surprise of the three men.

Sasha turned around and walked directly to the one who had said it. She stood in front of him with a frozen stare and stuck a finger inches from his face. "We are Persian, you moron, not Arabic, and we are American citizens. You need to be more respectful."

"Sorry," he mumbled.

Sasha turned back to a smiling Savanna and they practically skipped arm in arm up the steps to the main entrance. The three young men just stood there with stunned looks. Emma and Shane walked away smiling, both knowing the girls were going to be just fine.

Emma and Shane decided to have a cup of tea before going to see the bar owner, so they stopped in at a new little teahouse in Ballard. Shane opted for an Americano, which he loaded with sugar and a little cream. Emma got an organic black tea, and they settled into a table at the front of the room.

"So," said Shane. "There seems to be a significant part of the story that I have missed, like, I dunno, a person you killed, a Secret

Service protector, et cetera, et cetera." She looked at him with her eyes without turning her head, and took a sip of her tea, gently stirring it as she set it back down.

"Well," said Emma, "how much do you want to know? It gets pretty ugly."

Shane chuckled. "I'm all in at this point, so I might as well know the whole thing."

She took another sip of the tea. "I've already told you that my husband died in the war with Iraq. That was in early 1988, almost at the end of the war, as it turned out. I loved him very much, he was great man." She glanced around and lowered her voice. "When the man came with the letter telling me that my husband was dead, he tried to rape me, and I killed him with a knife and then went on the run. I was able to get a message out to a friend of mine who knew someone in the CIA, and they sent in a helicopter and rescued me and my daughters. We were very lucky to get out. A brave man died saving me and my daughters. It is a debt that I can never repay, other than to be the best person that I can be, and to try to instill the same values in my daughters."

She took a sip of tea and looked at Shane. She realized he had many of Eyelle's qualities: he was simple and very brave. "The CIA was convinced that my husband was involved in the nuclear program with Iran, because he had a nuclear engineering degree. They interviewed me endlessly, but I had no information for them. He was never involved in that, he was just fixing American equipment. He was doing it to save his country, not to help the regime, and the CIA could never understand that."

"But what about the witness protection part, what is that about?" asked Shane.

"Well, the Republican Guard were very serious about wanting to kill me for killing one of their own," Emma said. "They have many assassins around the world. It doesn't get a lot of press. A number of Iranian dissidents have been murdered, crimes that have been, quote unquote, 'unsolved.' No doubt it was by Iranian assassins. 8 years ago they almost killed me in France. I attended a meeting of Kurdish opposition leaders and there was a planned attack. Three Kurdish leaders were killed, I escaped through a bathroom window."

"Oh my God!" Shane exclaimed.

"I didn't have any information for the CIA, as my husband was not the bad guy they thought he was. They were most appreciative, however, that I killed Farzad Rostami, and so they agreed to help me stay alive. I was no longer Emma Aroundami, I was Emma Taylor. We have been able to avoid detection. I have already told you that I worked for a global health organization for many years, which was a big help. I was moved from location to location, and so I think it was difficult to find me. Now so many years have passed that I think I am not so much of a target, but I have been told that they still want to find me. But I don't lose sleep anymore. Whatever happens, happens. Ironically, the more terrorist things that happen, the safer I am, because it is getting much more difficult for Iranian bad guys to get here." Just then a young middle eastern looking man walked into the coffee shop. Emma instinctively followed his movements, then looked back at Shane.

"Are you worried they might go after the girls?" asked Shane.

"No, I don't believe that would happen. They want me, not the girls. The government there has its reasons for killing people, but they are calculated. It has military goals, their methods are not random. Killing innocents typically is not their way. Arab Sunnis are different, much more indiscriminate."

Shane wanted to ask the next question in the right way. "So how were you able to kill the guy?"

Emma took another sip of tea. She looked around a bit to make sure no one was listening, then looked at him with steely eyes. "He was slapping and punching me as he was trying to get my clothes off. I was fighting him as much as I could, but he was much stronger. I stumbled across the kitchen and into the counter, pulled a knife out of the block, flung it across the room, and hit him square in the chest."

She calmly pulled a sugar out of the holder and put it in her tea, gently stirring it, "I got lucky... he was about fifteen feet from me and I was going for a half spin, but it was more like three quarters. But I kept my knives very sharp and it seemed to hit just below his breastplate and caught a main heart artery, I guess. Fortunately, he had already mostly stripped and had taken off his heavy jacket. The knife went very deep."

Shane gave her a sober look. "Holy shit."

"Actually, when they picked me up with the CIA helicopter, there was another one, too."

"Another one?" asked Shane, not sure if he wanted to know.

"Yes, but I missed with the second one. I had some training from a guy in Seattle who ran a self-defense course. He was a Green Beret reserve, and ultimately he was recruited to be one of the guys on the helicopter that saved me, because he knew me. When you are being shot at while trying to escape at night in the middle of a forest from a bunch of people that want to kill you, it is very good to see a familiar face."

Shane chuckled at the understatement.

"One of my rescuers when I was escaping Iran was shot and paralyzed—I still stay in touch with him. It is hard for me not to cry, thinking about it all, but moving forward and staying strong for my girls has been a strong motivator. I don't think I would be alive if it wasn't for my girls."

Shane sat there drinking his coffee, shaking his head in disbelief.

"I do not regret killing the man who tried to rape me; he was pure evil. I do not believe he was a man of God. But the other men I do not know. They were just policemen, they could have been regular guys with families, who happened to be police officers. The man who drove me to the rendezvous, Eyelle, was executed right in front of me. He sacrificed his life for me and the girls, and he hardly knew us. There were so many sacrifices made for us, I don't even know the fate of some who helped. It is a burden that is hard to live with at times. I don't know if what happened is acceptable in the eyes of God; I just try to live a good life and provide guidance to my daughters."

She paused as a Muslim couple walked by on the sidewalk. They looked at Emma and smiled, and she nodded back.

Emma's casual tone in explaining her actions was the hardest thing for Shane to understand. As he sat there contemplating, he wasn't sure if he was crazy about this woman talking to him, or if she was just crazy. Either way, he thought a cold beer would sure taste good.

CHAPTER FORTY-FIVE

Emma had learned to be at peace with everything that had happened, and she was glad that Shane knew much of the story. Even the Kay policemen had to die for the girls to live and have a mother. Otherwise she would never have escaped, and she would likely have been killed on the spot.

She was already starting to plan the easiest way to get the car loaded and head back home. She was finally going to get some private time, and time to recover before going back to the clinic. It had been a crazy weekend, and she was so relieved that it was now close to over.

They stopped by the bank and she pulled out a thousand dollars to pay the bar owner. When they pulled into the parking lot they were able to see in the daylight where the car had backed into the building. A couple of men were working on the repairs, the smashed building sign lying off to the side.

They walked into the bar and found the owner working on straightening the place out. He looked up and saw them approach. "Well if it isn't Bonnie and Clyde."

Shane smiled but restrained his laugh. Emma was not amused. She handed him the envelope, saying, "Shane said you would be OK with a thousand dollars, and that it will all be kept quiet."

He looked at her and took the envelope. "Thank you for the cash and the understanding. Bar fights generally are not real good for business, nor helpful with my insurance rates."

"Yes," said Emma. "We would just prefer it go quietly away, I am very sorry this all happened." She and Shane turned to leave.

"One more thing," the man said. "It's kind of odd, but a fellow walked in earlier and handed me this." He handed Emma a plain white envelope, addressed to "the Middle Eastern woman in the bar fight."

Emma took the envelope and looked at it, shaken. "What did he look like?" asked Shane.

"Just an average, tall, thin, white guy. He had a red baseball cap on, I think it was a Red Sox hat. They're pretty good this year," said the bar owner.

Emma stared at the envelope, then looked up at the bar owner. "Thank you." She and Shane turned and left. As they walked out Shane said "I can't even guess what that is, but I don't have a great feeling about it."

"Neither do I," said Emma. "Let's wait until we get to your house to open it, just in case I have to scream or something." She shook her head. "I mean seriously, what else could happen this weekend?" Shane just chuckled and they headed home.

Emma sat down on the couch with the envelope in her hand. Something about it brought back terrible memories from sixteen years prior, and her hands trembled as she looked down at it.

"Just open it already," said Shane, who was working his way to the kitchen.

Emma nodded. "Yes, I'm sure you're right." She tore it open.

There was no salutation or letterhead. The note simply stated, "If you know who Hamid is, please follow these instructions exactly or you will never hear from me again. Call 206-276-2934 and leave a message with a date and time, nothing else. Use a public phone, do not use your own phone. At the date and time left in the message, I will be at Golden Gardens Park with a Boston Red Sox hat on, reading a book. Come alone. Do NOT leave anything on the message except the date and time."

Emma sat there staring at the note, stunned. Shane was in the kitchen, trying with one hand to open a beer. He glanced over at Emma's back and could tell something was wrong.

"Well, what is it?" he said, curiosity rising.

Emma just sat there staring, then frantically blurted, "How could he know Hamid's name? How is this possible? What is this?" Her voice rose as she threw the note down. She started walking around the room with her hands on her head, pulling her hijab off and pulling at her hair like a crazed woman. "Oh my God, oh my God, oh my God!"

Shane rushed over, picked up the letter and read it. "Easy, Emma. There has to be an explanation."

"Who have you told?" demanded Emma.

"No one, I swear. I don't think you even mentioned his name to me," said Shane, a bit frightened at her outburst. "Emma, calm down. We need to talk this through."

She stopped pacing. "OK, OK, I'm calm. Fine, I'm calm, now please tell me how he could know Hamid's name."

Shane looked at the letter again and tried to think. "OK, he doesn't know who you are or where you live, or it would have come to you rather than to the bar. He must have seen the picture in the paper and recognized you somehow; that's why he left it with the bar owner."

"Is he from Iran, here to kill me?" Her eyes were frantic.

"Well, he sure is picking a fairly public place for the assassination if that's the case." He realized too late that it wasn't a bit funny.

To his surprise, Emma actually took it well. "That is true, but why all the secret agent instructions?"

"I don't know, Emma. Should we go to the police or your Secret Service guy or something?"

"No," said Emma firmly. "I'm going to follow the instructions."

Shane sat on the couch, reading the letter again as Emma retrieved her hijab and put it back on, then went into the bedroom to regain her composure. Shane walked to the kitchen and put the beer back in the refrigerator. There was something about the name Hamid that was familiar to him.

"OK," said Shane as Emma returned to the living room. He took a deep breath and looked directly at her. "In for a dime, in for a dollar. We go together. I'll take my dad's snub-nose .38 in case he turns out to be an Iranian secret agent."

Emma tried to smile, but her chin trembled. "OK, I guess," she managed. "Where is the nearest public phone?"

CHAPTER FORTY-SIX

Emma called the phone number from a payphone at the nearby gas station. The call went directly to automated voicemail and she left a message saying that she would be in the designated park at seven p.m., in six hours. There would still be plenty of people in the park and sunset wouldn't be until after nine. She hoped the person would not be turned off by having Shane with her, but going alone seemed like too big a risk.

The afternoon went by very slowly as they discussed strategies and tried to reason out how this had happened, but nothing made any sense. Someone had recognized her and someone knew she was once married to Hamid. The secrecy part was disturbing, because it meant that it wouldn't just be some old college friend.

The time rolled around for them to head out. Shane got the gun, opened the chamber to make sure it was loaded, and expertly snapped it shut. He then tucked it gingerly into his arm sling so that it was well hidden.

"Do you have any experience with a gun?" asked Emma.

"Well, no secret agent stuff, no," said Shane. "But I know how to shoot, yes, although left-handed not so good. But these snub-nose 38's are only good for close range, anyway. After our little tearoom chat I'll feel better having a gun, is all. You have some pretty badass characters in your life."

Emma appreciated his easygoing attitude. Sometimes he was easygoing to the point of being dangerous, but he was very helpful right now.

"There's something else. I don't know if this is a great time to be bringing this up, but I'm thinking you need to know this," said Shane.

"Now what?" asked Emma.

"Look, I need a beer for this one." He went over and got the already-opened beer from earlier out of the fridge, took a long swig, and sat down at the table. Emma was at full attention.

"I did not put this all together until now, you must understand," Shane said.

"What, for fuck's sake!" Emma said, completely out of patience.

Shane took another swig and set the beer down firmly on the table. "Twenty-four or twenty-five years ago, I was a senior in high school, walking down Second Avenue toward Gas Works Park. I was minding my own business, then I heard this commotion going on in a yard. I looked over, and I see this young girl dive in between these two guys fighting."

Emma started shaking, staring at him wide-eyed. "Oh my God, oh my God," she mumbled.

Shane went methodically on. "If it's two guys I would probably have minded my own business and run away, I was just a kid. But I saw this young girl with a head scarf on dive in between two guys, one of them pounding the shit out of the other. Well, I didn't think, I just ran over and grabbed the bigger guy and pulled him off. We wrestled for a second, then I was standing there looking down the barrel of a gun. I begged him not to shoot me, I don't even remember what I said. The gun was two feet from my face, pointed right at me. He looked straight into my eyes, then turned the gun into his mouth and pulled the trigger. He blew his brains out right in front of me."

Shane looked out the window, took a deep breath, and continued. "I started running and I never stopped. I've still been running from that day. I didn't tell anyone—not my parents, not my friends, not the police, no one. I just kind of pretended it didn't happen all of these years. They didn't print the name of the girl in the paper because she was too young, but I remember the guy's name was Hamid."

The tears were streaming down Shane's face at this point. He was trembling, flashing back to the incident. He looked up at Emma and she was looking at him, shaking her head, tears flowing down her face as well.

Emma looked at him firmly and said, "It can only be God that has brought us together, that has brought you into my life. There is nothing else that explains this—it is impossible that this has all happened, that you were the one who saved our lives that day. That the car crash brought you to me, that the fight brought this note. This is all planned somehow; or it could not happen as it has happened."

Shane took a deep breath and blew out, wiped off his face, reached down and took another drink from the beer, then walked up to the sink and poured the rest out. "Yep, but God's got another chapter or two waiting for us. We need to get rolling."

CHAPTER FORTY-SEVEN

They arrived at the park to find a scattering of cars and people, typical for a warm weekday in Seattle. The long parking lot faced the beach looking west, which allowed them to drive slowly along the road to try to spot their mystery Red Sox fan. Benches were scattered between the beach and parking, with different family parties happening, kids and dogs running this way and that.

They made one pass of the lot without seeing anyone, then parked at a spot where they could see a long way in both directions. Shane then noticed a tall thin man with a reddish hat sit down on a picnic table at the far end of the parking lot. The man pulled a book out of his backpack and started to read.

"Is that him?" Shane asked, pointing. Emma looked, and saw that the man appeared to be reading, but was looking around every so often.

"Yes, I believe that is probably him." Her voice was steady but she was wringing her hands.

"Huh," said Shane, "this is surreal. At times I feel like this whole weekend has been one big dream."

Emma pinched him unexpectedly hard. Shane yanked his leg away. "Ow! No dream, I get it, ha ha," he said in an irritated voice.

Emma just continued to look toward the man. "Please come with me, but let me do the talking," she said firmly.

"OK then, here we go." They got out of the car and started walking toward the man. Emma had taken off her hijab for the first time in public in many years. Her outfit was the most casual American look that she could come up with. Not drawing attention to herself was the best strategy she could think of. Shane could not help but draw attention to himself, with his bruised face and arm sling.

As they approached, the man glanced their way and saw them, then turned back and focused on his book.

Emma and Shane cautiously approached to the other side of the bench and stopped, facing the man. Without looking up, the man said, "I told you to come alone. Who is he?" His pronounced southern twang came as a surprise.

"We thought you might be an Iranian agent here to kill me," Emma said.

The man snickered. "Do you still think this?"

"No. I think recruiting someone from Alabama to be an Iranian hit man would be very challenging."

Again the man snickered. "Georgia, actually." He hesitated, looked in both directions, and then looked directly into Emma's eyes and asked, "Are you the wife of Hamid Aroundami?"

Emma's knees started to give way. Shane helped her as best he could to the bench.

"I take that as a yes," said the man.

She nodded. "How-how do you know me, and how do you know who Hamid is? Who are you?"

"I can't tell you my name," he said, again looking around. "The information I'm about to give you is highly classified and I would basically be thrown into a brig for the rest of my life if I were found out. But I could not live out my life knowing what I know. I have not had a good night's sleep for two years." He wiped his face and gritted his teeth, obviously trying to keep his composure. "I have been on a search... I have been on a search... " he was struggling to get the words out. "For the wife of Hamid Aroundami."

"Why? Why have you been searching?" Emma demanded. "Did you know Hamid? You must have been a child when he died. I do not understand!" Her voice panicked.

The man took a deep breath. "In a nutshell, I have been on a search to clear my conscience. I was in the US Army Military Police in Iraq during the Gulf War, handling prisoners of special interest. Your husband was held in an Iraqi prison that we liberated during the Gulf War, then he was transferred into our custody as a high-value detainee. Once the war was over, he was moved to a variety of CIA black sites for a few years, then ultimately back to Guantanamo Bay, my last assignment."

Emma sat there blinking, not sure she understood. Finally she spoke in a quivering voice. "You are telling me that my husband is alive?"

The man looked back at her. "As of two years ago, yes ma'am, Hamid was alive. He was being held as a ghost prisoner at Guantanamo. It was too risky to let him go—he was too valuable, and there were too many rumors that he was associated with Iran's nuclear program."

"Oh my God." Emma's head collapsed to the table and she began crying in gasps.

"Ma'am, please try to control yourself," the man said. "I've got more information, and then I need to disappear."

Emma lifted her head and blew out a determined breath. "Yes, yes, please continue," she said, wiping her face. "Please tell me, what is a ghost prisoner, and what is a black site?"

"A ghost prisoner is one that has no name. No one knows they exist except the guards and interrogators. Even the heads of the

CIA and the president have little or no information. It's one of those plausible deniability situations set up with a blind eye to make sure that we hold on to those we consider high risk; it doesn't matter if they are guilty or not."

The man paused and looked down at the table, shaking his head. "Hamid had been labeled as being associated with the nuclear program in Iran, so once we had him we were not about to let him go. We couldn't let Iran know we had him, either, and they thought he was dead, so he ended up prisoner number A147/B. He was moved to a black site in Jordan, then to Egypt after the war ended, then ultimately to Guantanamo. He has been in isolation ever since."

"How do you know so much about him?" asked Emma, doing her best to keep her composure.

"I guarded him twice, first in Iraq for a while and again when he ended up back at Guantanamo. I wasn't CIA, just army military police. I was surprised to see him turn up again at Guantanamo—I figured he'd be long dead. We ended up having a lot of conversations, which is how I found out about you."

The man thought for a moment, looking at the ocean. "He would always be staring at the wall. I was just guarding him, never talking much to him. Obeying orders and protocol. One day I ask him something like, 'what in the hell are you looking at, man?' He continued to stare, so I got tough with him, you know, yelling at him. The staring was annoying." The man was struggling to tell the story, looking away and wiping his face. "He said, he said—," he was choking on his words. 'I am looking at Emma, can't you see her?'"

After a long pause to get his composure back, he added, "It was a moment in time for me. I realized that I was doing a bad thing. I was involved in something that I wanted no part of. I continued on for a while, talking with him as much as possible—too much, it turns out. One day my commander told me I was retiring, no other option, and that was the end of the army for me."

Emma was rocking gently back and forth, unable to speak. Shane looked at her and at the man, and said, "Unreal."

"So anyway," the man continued, "all I could find out was that you had killed an Iranian Revolutionary Guard and escaped Iran with your girls. It was one of those feel-good stories that got around, even though it was supposed to be kept at the highest level of secrecy. There were rumors that the CIA had picked you up and put you in a special protection program, but I was never able to get any information without raising suspicion, so I just let it be. I have just been kind of rambling in odd jobs for the last two years after I retired, looking at every publication or possible lead to try to find you, but I was starting to think that it would never happen. Hamid had mentioned you went to school in Seattle, so two months ago I moved here, just hoping I would run into you at a coffee shop, I guess. Then I saw the picture of that brawl with you and your daughters in the paper, and thought it was possible that it was you." He smiled. "And now you are sitting in front of me."

"Wow," said Shane. "Now what do we do?" Emma was still unable to speak.

"I can't publicly come forward, or admit that I've spoken to you, or I do hard time. This is the CIA's secret forced rendition program with about five layers of plausible deniability—no one will admit they know anything. The plan is, I suppose, to just keep Hamid in isolation until he dies, then bury him in an unmarked grave."

"Oh my God!" Emma exclaimed, burying her face in her hands.

"Sorry, that was pretty blunt. I suppose the best course would be to try to get someone in the CIA on your side, or perhaps an investigative journalist. It's unlikely anyone will admit to him being there, and only a few people even know about him... and I'm going to be brutally honest again: he could be dead at this point and no one would know that either. There are only a handful of people who know his name; he won't show up on any freedom of information lists or anything like that."

They sat there at the table, all of them just looking at each other, the reality of the situation sinking in. "The guards see these prisoners as animals and numbers," the man added. "If you show any compassion, they really don't want you guarding the dudes. No one wants to release anyone, because if they do and they really are a bad guy, it comes back to haunt the person that signed the release order. It's really a modern-day catch twenty-two, a no-win situation. Especially for the ghost prisoners like your Hamid. Who would sign a release order for someone who could build a nuclear bomb for Iran?"

"He had nothing to do with that program, it is absurd," said Emma, as if she was pleading for him to believe her.

"It's not about what he did or didn't do, it's about what the perception is. They can't prove his guilt or innocence, so they leave him there in isolation and nobody complains and no one has to make a decision that could hurt them politically. If no one knows he's there, there's no problem."

Emma was softly crying; it was all too much for her. She buried her head once again into her hands, trying not to make a scene.

"Perhaps I should have just let this be, not told you," said the man. "I don't know what is right and what is wrong anymore."

"Well, what do you think about Hamid?" said Shane.

The man met his eyes. "I have never met anyone like him. He has a calmness to him. Most men in isolation simply lose their minds, talk crazy and all. Not Hamid. He was kind and sympathetic, always asking about me and my problems, never complaining. I've heard about his wedding a hundred times, it's like I've been there." He turned to Emma. "Your face is exactly like he described."

The man shook his head as he looked at the sun lowering on the horizon, then added, "Some low-level idiot in the CIA labeled him as the nuke man of Iran, and now he is screwed."

"Will you help us?" said Emma, almost begging.

He took off his cap and ran a hand through his hair, then put it back on. "Ma'am, I don't want to go to jail, it's as simple as that. You're on your own at this point, and realistically, I don't think there is anything I can do. They would throw me in isolation so quick your head would spin. I think you must take the lead on this. I can be reached at that phone number that you called, it is a voice mail only. So you can phone me—that is the only thing I will agree to, and if there is some way that I can help that doesn't land me in jail, I would consider it. But if you try to track me down, I will deny ever talking to you." He looked Emma in the eye. "Now I'm going to get lost as best I can again, and I wish you well. I'm very sorry about all of this, and I apologize that I was involved. I'm pretty ashamed of the whole thing."

He stood up. Emma also stood, walked around the table and hugged him. "Thank you."

He nodded and walked away. Eventually they lost sight of him. Emma and Shane sat there at the table for a long time, staring at the now-setting sun.

CHAPTER FORTY-EIGHT

Sep 26, 2004, Washington, DC
CIA Director Jim Athan's office

"Good morning, sir," Assistant Director Kyle Hagen said as he walked in for the morning briefing.

"Good morning, Kyle," Director Athan said. "Let's get right to it. The president wants a briefing on our Guantanamo boys. He wants Bid Laden bad."

"Yes sir, I understand. I think we all do," said Kyle. "Coincidentally, we have kind of an odd issue that has popped up regarding Guantanamo."

"Talk to me," said the director. He had a bad feeling about what he was about to hear.

"Well, sir," said Kyle, "do you remember a woman named Emma Aroundami, the one we snatched out of Iran some sixteen years ago?"

"Yes, of course. I was directly involved in that one," said Athan.

"Well, sir, she's in the lobby, making a bit of a fuss," said Kyle.

Athan couldn't believe his ears. "What?" Said the director.

"Well, she has this wild idea that her husband, Hamid Aroundami, is being held by us at Guantanamo, and she wants to speak with you about it. She says she had a visit from one of his ex-guards."

The director looked at Kyle, stone faced. "OK, is there something I have missed here?"

Kyle took a deep breath and blew out, and said "Well sir, I cannot say for sure, and if I did know that we were holding him, it would be one of those examples of something best left unsaid."

"Shit," said Athan. "You have got to be kidding me."

"I wish I was," added Kyle quickly.

"OK," Athan said. "Let's say for argument's sake that there is someone who is potentially this person and we are holding him. What would his situation be?"

"Well, sir," said Kyle, "It could be that this guy was imprisoned during the Iran/Iraq war, only Iraq secretly kept him and a few others they considered high-value prisoners at the end of the war. Then we invaded a few years later, found him and thought he might be involved in Iran's nuclear program. Rather than sending him back to Iran, we decided to keep him in the system. All hypothetical, of course."

Athan buried his head in his hands and said, "Oh Judas H. Priest, I can't believe this."

"It is my opinion, sir, that we deny all knowledge of his existence, put him on the next plane to Egypt, and the problem is solved," Kyle said without emotion.

The director looked at Kyle and shook his head. "This is one of the parts of this job that I hate." He sat there thinking for a moment, nervously tapping the desk. "I'm not going to do that. I'm going to bring this to the president's attention at my meeting this morning, let him make the call... fuck it. We did everything possible to get this woman out years ago, now we turn around and secretly get rid of her husband and deny we ever knew anything? Not on my watch. Get me the file on Aroundami ASAP."

"Actually, sir, you will not see that name anywhere. He is officially prisoner number A147/B," said Kyle.

"Whatever, Kyle, just get me the goddamn file," said the director, clearly irritated. "Tell Mrs. Aroundami that I will meet her this afternoon, and ask her to please stay quiet in the meantime."

"Yes sir, I will take care of it," responded Kyle.

CHAPTER FORTY-NINE

Director Athan arrived at the president's office, not sure how he was going to present his problem. When he entered the room, the president was on the phone, and Athan greeted Chief of Staff Ed Saunders quietly as the president finished his conversation. Athan's thoughts wavered on what to do, but he kept going back to common decency and doing the right thing. Nothing had turned up in sixteen years that connected Aroundami to Iran's nuclear program; the file was all innuendo and speculation. Aroundami had held firm that he was just helping to rebuild American equipment during the war with Iraq, and his story was believable. The problem now was that he had been held way too long to just let him go.

The president hung up. "Good day, Jim, I hope this will be a short meeting. I'm heading to Camp David with the family later."

"Yes, sir," said Jim. "Mostly routine items, with one exception." He handed the president a manila folder.

The president looked at him quizzically. "OK, fire away. What's the exception?"

"Well, it involves that Aroundami woman we rescued from Iran sixteen years ago."

"Yes," said the president. "The one who killed Farzad Rostami. Quite a story. I know all about it, I've been quite a student of our success stories, that one caught my attention when I was briefed early on."

"Yes, sir. Well, we changed her name, gave her some Secret Service protection to keep her from being assassinated by the Iranians, and thought it was the end of the story. Then this morning I get word that she is under the impression that we are holding her husband, Hamid Aroundami, at Guantanamo Bay. I have an appointment with her after our meeting."

The president looked up, surprised. "Really. OK, so are we holding Hamid Aroundami?"

"Well, sir, prisoner number A147/B fits his description."

The president shook his head. "Shit."

"Yes sir, my reaction as well," said Jim. "Turns out he was captured by the Iraqis during the war with Iraq and held. They didn't give him back to Iran after the war because they thought he was too valuable. We liberated the remaining Iranians when we went in, but we held him as a ghost prisoner, mostly in Egypt and Jordan, because we thought he was part of Iran's nuclear program."

"And is he?" asked the president.

"We have never been able to establish that link, but no one wanted to take the chance, so he became prisoner number A147/B and has been held mostly in isolation ever since. The Egyptians got tired of holding him because we wouldn't let them kill him, and they didn't want to be holding an Iranian. We moved him around, but he was too hot for some of our allies to keep because we wanted him alive for intelligence reasons, and they didn't want to be holding an Iranian national either. So a couple of years ago we transported him to Guantanamo as prisoner number A147/B. He had no terrorist links that we have been able to find, he just kind of ended up there... we simply never connected the dots."

"And what is the plan now?" asked the president.

"Well, we really don't have a plan other than to just hang on to him. Everyone thought he was dead until now."

"Wow," said the president, again shaking his head. "Just tell me one thing, Jim. Is he Al Qaeda, or not?"

"Well sir, he's Iranian, so highly unlikely," said Jim, confused by the president's question.

"You're telling me that there aren't any Iranians in Al Qaeda?"

"Sir," said Jim, as respectfully as possible, "Al Qaeda is primarily Sunni, the Iranians are primarily Shiite, and most of the funding for Al Qaeda is coming from Saudi Arabia, as best as we can tell. The Iranians and Al Qaeda just don't like each other very much."

The president looked at Jim, then said slowly and firmly, "Is the man a risk to the citizens of this country?"

"Well, sir, it is my opinion that he is what he has always said he is, and that he was helping to rebuild the leftover American equipment for their fight against Iraq. I don't think there is anything else from a military standpoint, but it would be awfully embarrassing to release him at this point. But no sir, I do not believe he is any kind of a risk. There is more to the story, however."

"Go on," the president said.

"Well," said Athan, "We've been moving him around because no one wants to guard him... not just that, it's like no one wants to be the one interrogating him."

The president was confused. "You're going to have to be clearer than that, Jim. What exactly are you talking about?"

"Well, sir," Jim continued. "It's like he is some sort of savant—he has some sort of unique attraction. We've had battle-hardened interrogators request to be released from working with him, guards have quit or retired, it's like no one wants to be responsible. I can't explain it. The Egyptians were flat-out afraid of the guy; they demanded that we take him."

"So he's an Islamic radical, one of those guys that stirs everyone up?" asked the president.

"No, no, just the opposite. He doesn't even really act like the rest of them. He doesn't pray like they do, just kind of sits cross-legged in his cell, staring at the wall. But everyone wants to know if Hamid is well, if Hamid is safe, if Hamid is alive. Not just the prisoners—the guards, the staff, anyone who has ever been in contact with him. The file on him is bizarre, there's no other way to describe it. Even though he is supposed to be a ghost, the word has gotten out that he exists. On more than one occasion, the guards working with him have asked that he be released. One of our top interrogators went insane, there's no other way to describe it. The guy lost his mind and is now in North Carolina in a mental institution. I even had a call from our contact in Egypt—the guy is a brutal bastard and as heartless as they come. He just wanted to know if Hamid was still alive."

The president stood and started pacing back and forth, the two other men in the room eyeing him nervously.

"Another thing, sir," Athan went on. "We're pretty sure he is dying. He weighs about a hundred pounds, but he is still eating. It's like he's burning through his food. The doctors down there have no idea what is happening."

The president continued to pace, then he stopped and leaned back against his desk, facing the two men.

"Ed, what's your opinion?" Asked the president.

The chief of staff shrugged. "We could release him into her custody," he suggested. "She is, and always will be, hiding from the Iranians. I don't see how this hurts us, politically or otherwise. I think we should keep it as quiet as possible, but even if the story came out it would seem like we were doing the right thing."

The president turned to Athan. "Jim, your thoughts?"

"I don't see an intelligence risk," Athan said. "He is sixteen years out of the loop, barely alive. Besides, it's unlikely that he's going to want to help the people who want to kill his wife. They don't want publicity any more than we do."

The president sat back down at his desk and started flipping through the file, but not really reading anything. "Ed", he said, "Come up with a plan, please."

"OK," said Saunders. "We send her down to Guantanamo tonight on a private plane and release Aroundami. We tell Mrs. Aroundami that we want everything quiet for her security and for his. We offer them a reasonable financial settlement that we can justify if this comes out."

"Fine," said the president. "Jim, make it happen."

"Yes, sir. I was hoping that would be your response. I think this is the right thing to do," said Jim.

The president stared at him coldly. "I hope it is too. If we're wrong it would be pretty ugly. But if we can find ways to reduce the numbers down there without increasing our risk, I'm willing to listen."

"Thank you, sir," said Jim.

"OK, let's move this along, I want to get to Camp David, I need a vacation. And Jim, one more thing. Tell Mrs. Aroundami we are real sorry about this."

CHAPTER FIFTY

Jim returned to his office, eager to get the Aroundami mess cleaned up as quickly as possible.

Kyle entered with a file in his hand and sat down in front of the director. "Mrs. Aroundami will be returning at two p.m. There is a fellow with her that looks like he's been through a windshield or something. Apparently he has been helping her out. I'm not sure what it means, considering the looks of the guy, but I think he knows about Hamid as well. Somebody has spilled the beans."

"OK," said the director. "We're going to let Aroundami go."

"Sir?"

"We're going to let him go," Athan repeated. "I've got the president's go ahead. Do you have any other bits to the puzzle we need to know about?"

Kyle shrugged. "I'm not sure we can keep this quiet. If the press gets ahold of it, someone will win the Pulitzer for exposing us."

"We'll make it clear to Mrs. Aroundami that we would prefer that not happen—no threats, but we would prefer that neither of them have any contact with Iran or the press. This needs to be kept a private matter."

Kyle thought for a moment. "Well, again, there's no chance she'll go back to Iran. She would be executed. And he's probably a train wreck after spending sixteen years in isolation. I'm sure he's been through hell."

The director picked up the phone. "Alice, please get me the base commander at Guantanamo on the line, and please arrange a small private jet for a trip to the base this evening. We'll also need a liaison and a couple of civilian guards."

CHAPTER FIFTY-ONE

Emma and Shane were shown into Director Athan's office. When they entered, the director and Kyle both stood. The director walked around his desk to greet Emma.

"Emma, it has been a while." He waited for her to extend her hand—he was never sure what to do with women in hijabs. She initiated the handshake, surprising the director with a very strong grip. Jim had been the initial person interviewing Emma upon the return from Iran, although others did most of the interrogation.

"Hello, Mr. Athan. This is my friend Shane Merrill."

"My pleasure." The director shook Shane's left hand and motioned them to their seats.

"Emma, before you begin, I'm just going to dive in here and let you know what is happening. First, you must believe that we had never connected the dots on your husband. I didn't know that he was in our detention."

Emma was stunned. She had been expecting a battle, and was prepared to demand that her husband be released. She had assumed they would deny and deny. So she couldn't even comprehend what the director had said. She glanced over at Shane and saw him with the same dazed and confused look he'd had when she'd walked in on the girls dancing in front of him.

"What?" Emma said.

"Your husband," said the director. "He has been held at Guantanamo as prisoner A147/B for the last couple of years. The name never crossed my desk, or at least I missed it if it did. I did not know he was Hamid Aroundami. However, now I know, and I have received approval from the president to release him to your custody on the condition that this be kept a private matter for national security reasons, and that neither you nor your husband ever go back to Iran. If you agree to the terms, you will receive a financial compensation package that should make life easier, and you will have mine and the president's sincerest apologies for this whole affair. We have arranged transportation to Guantanamo for you and your friend—we will fly you there this evening. We will need you to sign some paperwork first, then the plane can take you all back to Seattle. He is free to go."

The last thing Emma remembered before collapsing was, "He is free to go."

CHAPTER FIFTY-TWO

The door to Hamid's cell opened unexpectedly. Normally there would be shouted instructions prior to entering. Never could he remember the door simply opening.

He stared up at the man, irritated. He never liked being taken away from the vision of his Emma. But he could not understand what he was seeing. The man was in civilian clothing—a suit and tie—and two guards stood behind him. The guards would usually be in front, and he could never remember seeing a man in a suit.

"Mr. Aroundami," the man said.

"What, you know my name now?"

He knew his rudeness would likely lead to punishment, but it was such an odd thing to hear his name.

"Yes, we know your name. Please, come with us," said the man.

"Are you going to kill me now, after all this time? Why didn't you just kill me when I arrived? Why didn't you let the Egyptians kill me?" he demanded.

The man looked sideways at Hamid, with a confused look. "We are not going to kill you, Mr. Aroundami. You are being released.

Please come with us so that we can get you into some civilian clothes." He gestured for Hamid to follow him. Hamid was just staring, sure he had not heard the man correctly. Your mind plays many tricks on you in isolation, he thought. It is a torture that is beyond comprehension, for those who have not endured it.

But he had come up with a way to fight off insanity, to keep his mind going, to keep his will to live, and that was his Emma. He remembered an American book that she had read to him to work on his English, about a man who was being tortured, but who felt no pain because he would always take his mind away, and spend the hours with his love. So Hamid had used that strategy throughout the years of his imprisonment; there was not a moment that went by that he did not think of Emma. He would constantly remind himself of her voice, practicing it in his mind over and over so he would not forget.

His favorite thing to do was to sit and stare at the wall of his cell. Her reflection in the mirror at their wedding would appear, as clear as the day they were married. Every feature of her face he could see in the concrete wall, just as if she were sitting next to him. She would have on her beautiful wedding dress, the hijab fluttering backward, and her beautiful green eyes were looking directly into his.

When the hours turned into days and the days turned into years, he would imagine her hands—how he loved her hands. He would see her hand as she laid it on his. He could send his mind to walking with her in the park, a lovely walk that they would do every day, hand in hand. They would look at the trees, the birds, smell the air, and just be with each other. The walk never ended, in his mind. Even through the unspeakable brutality of some of the places he had been, they would always go on their walks together.

So he had never been lonely or scared in captivity; Emma was always there to comfort him. Sometimes they would sit and have tea together, the cardamom-and-rosewater tea that Emma made that he loved so much. They would just sit there, drinking tea and listening to the birds.

After his interrogations, Hamid greatly looked forward to being back in the isolation cell, as he would send himself to Emma's side, no longer distracted by his tormentors. She was always there for him, and he for her, in an endless path of beauty and perfection. At times he would be so lost in his mind that he would think he had actually died and gone to heaven, and this was what it would be like for eternity. Then he would be rudely snapped out of it by one of his tormentors, who would try again to pry some non-existent information out of him.

But once back in isolation, it was back to his Emma, and all was right again. He had lost the ability to distinguish whether he was awake or asleep years ago, his time alone in the cell was a blur of visions. In fact, he and Emma had been on a lovely walk when the man in civilian clothes asked him to come with them.

Hamid was not afraid of his execution; he was ready for his own death. He knew that it meant that he would be with his Emma at some point in the afterlife, and at least he would be free of his tormentors.

But if they were taking him to his death, this was an odd way to do it. So odd, in fact, that he could not help saying, matter-of-factly, "Why do I need civilian clothes to be executed? I am perfectly happy to be killed in these clothes."

The man in civilian clothing seemed shocked. "I... " he hesitated. "I don't know how to put this in a way that you will understand. I know that you have been through hell. You are being released to the custody of your wife, Emma Aroundami. She is on her way here now, and you will be leaving on a plane for Seattle later this evening."

Hamid stood there looking at the man, this well-dressed man who was telling him the cruelest lie he possibly could before sending him to his death. The cruelty of these people knew no bounds.

"Fine, take me where you will, I am ready," he said strongly. They walked together through the main yard, Hamid preparing his mind for death. He could not understand why they had not bound his hands—perhaps this was actually some odd dream that he was in, walking across the yard with a man in civilian clothes and two guards, and he was walking with them instead of being shoved and dragged by them. What an odd dream, he thought.

They all walked through a door that he had not been through before. This must be the room where it happened. Perhaps it would be a simple gunshot, but then, he had never heard gunshots, and he didn't think that was how they did it.

"In that room you will find a suit, and there is a shower and shaving kit," the man said, pointing to a door at the rear of the room. "She will be here soon, please get ready."

So they are doing it like they did with the Jews? They make me feel all safe and put out clothes for me, then send poison through the shower? What an odd thing to do. Hamid's mind raced to come up with why they would kill him that way, but he was not going to give them the satisfaction. The razors supplied would be perfect. He would just break the plastic off, slit his wrists, then turn on the shower. He would take his own life. That way they would know that he knew, and that he had beaten them to the execution.

CHAPTER FIFTY-THREE

When Emma woke she was on the couch in the back of the director's office. A medic was there checking her vitals.

"Mrs. Aroundami, please take these pills, they will help." She took the pills and drank some water from the glass he held out, not questioning what they were or why she was there. The people in front of her seemed to know what they were doing.

It finally came to her where she was. "I'm sorry, I passed out," was all she could say.

"Yes, we knew that," said Shane, smiling at her. "It's true, Emma. They have Hamid and he is being released. You'll need to sign some non-disclosure documents. I will go with you if you want. I'll leave it up to you, but we need to get you ready to make this happen."

She drank some more water, then thought for a moment. "Yes, come with me. I need the support, if you don't mind."

"In for a dime, in for a dollar," said Shane, winking at her.

"I need to call the girls," Emma said.

The plane was a small Lear jet. They all climbed the steps and boarded. "This is how the other half lives," Shane said as they entered the jet, which was smartly decorated, with plenty of food and drink. Shane was very pleased to see some Northwest beers on offer. Soon they were heading south from the capital for the three-hour flight to Guantanamo Bay. It was all happening so fast that it was hard to believe it was real. They were accompanied by two security guards and an official from the director's office who was assigned to help them through the steps, and also to brief them on what to expect.

"My name is Janice Wynn," she said. She was a sharply dressed woman in a pant suit with a leather shoulder bag that looked like a briefcase. "I will be your liaison through this. We will pick up your husband at Guantanamo, then fly with you to Seattle. We should arrive late tomorrow morning. The guards are here in case your husband has psychotic episodes, for everyone's safety aboard. The reality is that there will be a very long adjustment period. We don't know what kind of shape he is in. You will, of course, have access to counseling and full medical benefits. I will be available for any help you need; they have given me authorization to do what it takes."

Just then, Emma closed her eyes. She felt something terrible was happening. Her mind went ablaze, everything around her disappeared. Suddenly she screamed, "Stop!" stunning everyone in the plane.

"Emma," Shane said softly, "Emma, it's OK. Are you alright?"

Her eyes were still closed until the sensation stopped, then she opened them and looked around. "I'm sorry, I just felt something terrible was happening, I need to rest."

"Of course, of course," a startled Ms. Wynn said.

Emma felt a calming sensation as she closed her eyes again. She instantly fell asleep, and she was with Hamid. They were on the path that they had been on every night for the last sixteen years, only now Hamid was standing at the edge of a cliff. He stopped just before falling off and looked back at her. She held out her hand and he looked at it, but seemed unsure what to do. He slowly lifted his hand and she took it and pulled him back from the edge of the cliff. His face was worn, his body thin and frail; she could see that he was dying.

When she was woken out of the dream, tears were streaming down her face.

"Emma, Emma!" Shane was gently nudging her. "Are you OK?" He could see the tears pouring from her eyes and was trying his best to be gentle. "We will be landing soon."

CHAPTER FIFTY-FOUR

"Stop!" Was all Hamid heard in his mind as he started to press the razor into his wrist. He was startled by the voice: it was Emma. He could not understand why she would want him to stop. Wouldn't his death mean that they would be together that much sooner? Hamid then heard knocking on the door, but he could not move. He was curled up in a corner of the room, completely naked, and he had lost control of his bowels. But none of this mattered to him.

He was hearing voices and cursing, but was now floating in a surreal world between life and death. He knew he was going to die, either by his own hand or at the hands of his captors, and maybe he was already there. There was more cursing, and he thought that he must still be alive, that there wouldn't be this much cursing in heaven. He felt the warm water flow over him, and arms holding him upright. The arms holding him weren't causing pain, which had always been the case. Instead, they were just holding him upright.

He could feel a brush scrubbing his body, which was painful but nothing like what he had been through, and it felt good to have the warm, soapy water running across his skin. He still had no strength in his legs, and soon he was sitting on a chair, slumped and groggy. He could feel towels drying his body, and instructions that he had no strength to follow.

He had nothing left. After sixteen years in captivity, he was ready to die. The last bit of strength and mental awareness had been stolen from him as he prepared his mind for his death—he could not understand why Emma had not let him take his own life. Soon he felt clothes on him, but did not have the strength to open his eyes.

The men in the room picked him up and moved him to another room where there was a couch, and they propped him upright. He could hear voices but still could not open his eyes.

"What are we going to do?" He could hear them talking a little better than before, as his mind came back a bit. There were several voices.

"We can't release him like this, for fuck's sake."

"We don't have a choice. Can we get some coffee in him, or something? What kind of stimulant will help?"

"I'm afraid anything we give him will kill him."

Hamid feebly raised his hand, and whispered, "Please, no drug."

The room went silent. The men were standing around Hamid, and all had a new appreciation for the broken man in front of them. They had all witnessed, at one point or another, the psychological torture he had been through here, and they all knew what he must have been through in Egypt. Sixteen years... they were all silently appreciative of the strength the man must have had, just to make it this far.

"No more drugs, Hamid, you are a free man," one of the men said. "Can you drink a bit of coffee?" The man speaking brought a warm cup to Hamid's mouth, and he was able to sip a bit. As the liquid entered his mouth, Hamid was able to open his eyes a crack.

There was a knock at the door. The men in the room all looked at each other as one said, "Here we go."

They opened the door to two civilian guards, a woman in a hijab, and another beat-up man with an arm sling. Emma pushed her way through the guards and dropped to her knees in front of Hamid, putting her hands on his legs and dropping her head into his lap, crying inconsolably.

The first bit of realization hit Hamid. This was Emma in front of him. The tears were rolling out of his eyes, but he could not form words; he was just looking and trying to grasp the whole situation. Finally, he lifted his hand slightly and placed it over hers. "My sweet love," he whispered.

A man said, "Let us help you get him to the plane."

"NO! Keep your hands off him!" Emma screamed, shocking the men back a few steps. She started to help him up as best she could. The other men in the room stayed back, except for the beat-up one, who moved forward and slipped his good arm under Hamid's arm. Together, the three of them were able to stand and shuffle their way to the door.

The guards from the plane were holding the door open as they made their way out, never looking back at the men in the room. Hamid felt that he was in the presence of love holding him up for the first time in sixteen years, and it gave him strength. He was able to move his legs slightly as they walked through the darkness to the plane.

When they reached the steps to the plane, the guards carefully asked Emma, "Ma'am, can we help a bit?"

"Yes, thank you," Emma said, and they were able to get Hamid into the plane. He was asleep before they were all settled in, the exhaustion and confusion taking its toll.

As the sun was just starting to rise above the horizon, he woke to the smell of cardamom tea, a smell he had not experienced for over sixteen years, other than in his dreams.

Emma brought a cup to his lips. "Do you remember, sweet man?" He sipped the tea she was holding and motioned for more, and she stroked his head. She brought a biscuit to his mouth. He bit into it, and immediately recognized it as his favorite Madar honey biscuit—something he almost had forgotten existed. He eagerly ate the rest of the biscuit and found strength in the loving nourishment.

He was able to sit up on his own, and look around at his odd surroundings. There was a woman and two men who looked like guards or policemen near the back, Emma was sitting nearest him, and the man with the sling and bruises was sleeping near the front.

"How is it that I am here?"

"It is a long story, my love, but we will have much time to explain. You need your strength now. Your daughters will be meeting us at the airport soon."

His daughters. He could not speak, he just started crying. Emma sat next to him and he collapsed onto her shoulder.

They landed at a private strip north of Seattle. As the door opened, Hamid said, "Please, let me go alone." He started toward the exit, bracing himself on the seats. The girls were hurrying toward the plane. When they spotted him at the top of the stairs they broke into a dead sprint, purses and belongings scattering as they went. He had made it to the bottom of the stairs when they reached him. "Daddy, daddy, daddy," they cried, sobbing and hugging him uncontrollably.

Both girls wore flowing head scarves. Hamid had never before witnessed such beauty. Emma joined them at the bottom of the stairs, and they all slowly walked together to the waiting car, taking turns helping Hamid.

Emma turned back toward Shane, who had been following at a respectful distance. She came up to him and smiled gently. "We can perhaps get together another time for introductions—obviously, there is a lot of healing that needs to happen. I cannot begin to express my gratitude. I will gladly pay for a taxi."

Shane smiled at her. "It's all good, no need, I'll find my way home. It was a fun weekend," he added. They both smiled at the obvious understatement. She placed her hand over her heart and smiled at him, then turned and headed back to the car.

Shane looked around, noticed a sports bar across the street from the airfield, and headed that way. He thought there might be a morning baseball game about to start, and he could really use a burger and a beer.

The end.